Coming in July from

ODD MAN OUT #505
by Lass Small

*Roberta Lambert is too busy with her job to notice that her
new apartment-mate is a strong, desirable man. But Graham
Rawlins has ways of getting her undivided attention....*

Roberta is one of five fascinating Lambert sisters. She is as
enticing as each one of her three sisters, whose stories you have
already enjoyed or will want to read:

- Hillary in GOLDILOCKS AND THE BEHR (Desire #437)

- Tate in HIDE AND SEEK (Desire #453)

- Georgina in RED ROVER (Desire #491)

Watch for Book IV of Lass Small's terrific miniseries and read
Fredricka's story in TAGGED (Desire #528) coming in
October.

CATHRYN CLARE
Blind Justice

Silhouette Desire

Published by Silhouette Books New York

America's Publisher of Contemporary Romance

SILHOUETTE BOOKS
300 East 42nd St., New York, N.Y. 10017

ISBN: 0-373-05508-0

First Silhouette Books printing July 1989

Printed in the U.S.A.

To Ellen,
my partner in crime

Books by Cathryn Clare

Silhouette Desire

To the Highest Bidder #399
Blind Justice #508

CATHRYN CLARE

is a transplanted Canadian who moved south of the border when she married a far-from-proper Bostonian four years ago. While she's thought of herself as a writer since she wrote her first poem at the age of six, she's also been a musician, storyteller and orchestra manager. She met her husband, a trumpet player, on a winter tour of Northern Ontario: "We were cooped up together on a bus for a week," she says, "and things turned out just about the way you'd expect them to in a romance novel!"

One
___

"Close checking account," Lily Martineau muttered, half out loud to herself. "Take the garbage downstairs. Give the rubber plant back to the landlady."

She was standing at a traffic-clogged intersection in downtown Boston, waiting for the light to change. Most pedestrians were ignoring the lights, dodging cars as they crossed the street, but Lily had an ingrained habit of waiting for the walk signal. She'd always had that law-abiding streak in her. Perhaps it was one of the things that had prompted her to become a lawyer.

"Make sure the oven's clean." The light seemed to be taking longer than usual today, but no doubt she was just impatient to be gone. Why were there so many things to think about on moving day? "Mail the change-of-address cards I just picked up at the post office. Call Sarah to tell her what time I'm arriving in Hartford."

She looked across the street, to the bulky Massachusetts courthouse. It was half-hidden behind a new office tower, but even without seeing the open plaza in front of it, she could picture its usual hustle and bustle. It felt odd that all the people she'd worked with for the past year were gone now. Most of her friends had been law clerks like herself, and they'd moved away to take jobs elsewhere.

Now it was her own moving day. She'd been looking forward to this all year long. In her imagination she'd always seen herself signing on as a junior, yet important, member of a small, dedicated law firm somewhere. But instead she had accepted a short-term contract working for a big insurance firm in Hartford, simply because she had to eat and pay rent while she was looking for that perfect small law firm. It probably built character to compromise once in a while, she thought.

"Call the moving company at one-thirty to make sure they're still on for three o'clock. Pick up my good suit at the cleaners." Lily had been concentrating so hard on her list, she didn't notice the blind woman until she was halfway across Tremont Street. The wizened little woman with her white cane was tentatively tapping her way toward Lily through the crowded intersection.

Lily had always thought that the Boston pedestrian, as a species, was mainly concerned about self-preservation, and seeing no one in the surging stream of people giving any thought to the blind woman only confirmed Lily's opinion. She had a sudden sense of how it must feel to be groping your way through a darkness that was filled with hurrying people and impatient drivers.

I'm in a hurry, too, Lily thought, but the light's about to change again and that poor woman is heading off into the middle of the street. She hurried to the blind woman's side.

"Which way are you headed?" she asked, putting a hand on the woman's arm.

She was expecting a grateful answer, but instead she found her hand shaken off and heard a cantankerous reply. "There's no need to touch me!" the woman said tartly. "I was doing just fine."

Lily took a quick look around. The walk signal was flashing orange, and in a moment they'd be in the firing line for three lanes of traffic. "The light just changed," Lily informed the blind woman. "You'd better hurry up."

The woman couldn't have been more than five feet tall—Lily, at five six, felt like a towering giant next to her—but every inch of her was rooted to the spot, and a very uncomfortable spot it was becoming. Traffic had started to move, and Lily could hear horns honking as drivers let their feelings be known.

"How can I hurry," the woman demanded, "when you've got me all turned around? I don't know which way I was going now."

"You need to turn a bit to your left," Lily said. Grant me patience! she thought. The woman seemed to be in her seventies; it was a miracle she'd survived that long if she made a habit of picking fights in the middle of downtown intersections. "You'll have to wait a minute," Lily added. "There's a line of cars between us and the curb now."

The woman waved her cane at the traffic she couldn't see. "Shame on them!" she cried, and Lily could have sworn she sounded pleased about it. "Don't you know pedestrians have the right of way?"

Lily could hear the exasperation in her own voice. "Maybe this isn't the best time to lecture them about the rules of the road," she said. "Look, this man's going to let us through. If we hurry, we can do it." She reached for the woman's elbow again to guide her through the gap.

The woman's reaction was as fierce and immediate as before. "Get your hands off me!" she cried. Her voice was wizened like the rest of her, an old voice with cracks in it. "No one asked you to touch me, young woman!"

The motorist who had stopped to let them through was waving at them now, urging them to cross, and Lily waved back helplessly, trying to convey her predicament. The man shrugged and then drove on, no doubt tired of listening to the chorus of horns behind him.

This was ridiculous. Lily had an amused vision of how they must look, the old woman in a shapeless red dress and Lily in her oldest jeans and a baggy navy blue sweatshirt—her housecleaning garb. They probably appeared to be two bag ladies tussling in the middle of the street.

Lily took a grip on herself and schooled her naturally gentle voice into the professional sound she'd developed. "I'll argue with you all you want when we get to the sidewalk," she said firmly, "but this isn't the time or the place."

Instead of holding the woman's elbow this time, she settled for a guiding hand on her back, hoping that wouldn't count as "touching." Surely the woman must realize there wasn't another way to show a blind person which way to go! She obviously needed help; then why was she being so adamant in refusing it?

Lily's professional voice didn't work this time. The old woman recoiled as though she'd been burned, and stepped away, seeming determined to find her own way. But she moved so quickly that she lost her balance, and before Lily could reach out or call a warning, the woman had taken a crooked half step backward and reeled into the next lane of traffic. There was a horrifying squeal of brakes, quickly drowned out by a blast from a horn. Lily involuntarily shut her eyes tight, and when she opened them again, the old woman was lying in a heap on the pavement and the shining black vehicle that had hit her had come to a screeching halt.

Lily blinked, wanting to make the scene go away, but it was too obviously real. Other drivers were stopping to look, the horns' blaring had escalated into a full symphony, and a man had erupted out of the black Jeep and was adding his voice to the fray.

"What the hell were you doing, pushing her into the traffic?" he was demanding, and Lily realized with a start that he was talking to her. "I didn't have a chance to stop, never saw her until she was right under the wheels."

A sharp reply rose to Lily's lips, but before she could answer, the man knelt down by the blind woman, and Lily was left staring at the russet top of his head instead of his handsome, angry face. You couldn't very well confront the top of someone's head, she thought irrationally, and realized that she wasn't quite as much in command of herself as she might be.

This won't do, she told herself firmly. There was no need for her to stand there gaping while the man who'd caused the accident simply took over. Quickly she knelt down on the pavement next to him and was mightily relieved to see that the blind woman was still breathing, although she seemed to be unconscious.

A crowd had gathered already, and Lily heard someone shout that he would go into the church on the corner and call an ambulance.

"We'd better not move her," she cautioned. "You don't know what might be broken."

The auburn-haired man gave her a look of pure contempt. "Thank you for that valuable advice," he said sarcastically. "You must watch a lot of doctor shows on TV."

Lily's breath caught in her throat, and her sudden anger seemed to clear her brain. "And you must watch a lot of police shows," she shot back. "Especially the chase scenes, or do you always drive like that?"

She almost wished she hadn't said it. The man's head whipped up to face her, and she found herself at the receiving end of a brown-eyed glare. "I drive," he said slowly and distinctly, "as safely as anyone I know. Unfortunately, when people get pushed under my wheels, there's not much I can do about it."

There was something disturbing in the way their angry gazes had locked. It wasn't just that the stranger was leveling an unjust accusation at her. Something about him brought out every fighting instinct she had.

He was a big man, and maybe that had something to do with it. His broad shoulders and obvious strength dwarfed her just as Lily had dwarfed the old blind woman a few minutes before. Was he using his size to intimidate her, or was he always so aggressively male? Lily couldn't tell, but she was busy calling up all the tricks she'd learned in the past few years when faced with domineering men.

The stranger had on an expensive-looking tweed suit, and Lily wished she wasn't wearing her very oldest, baggiest sweatshirt. It was much easier to stand up to opposition when you were well dressed, she'd discovered. Still she couldn't just let him point the finger of blame at her.

She sat back on her heels, knowing there was nothing else she could do for the old woman until the ambulance arrived. "I don't know what you're getting at," she said to the stranger, "but if you think I was responsible for this, you can think again. I was just trying to help this lady out."

"Some help!" the man said, clearly scornful. He had to raise his voice to be heard over the car horns behind them where traffic was backing up in a serious way. Lily had the strange image of the three of them and the man's black Jeep being a little island in the midst of a sea of cars.

The old woman made a half-conscious movement, and Lily thought she heard a low moan from her lips. In an instant she shelved her anger at the man beside her. That could come later; right now the injured woman was more important.

"You'll be all right," she said on the chance that the woman was conscious enough to hear. "There's an ambulance coming."

The answering moan was stronger this time, and Lily reached out to take the woman's hand. She could feel a slight squeeze in response. It must be terrifying to waken in a dark and noisy world, Lily thought. No doubt anybody's touch was a comfort at this point, no matter what phobia the woman had shown earlier about Lily's guiding hand.

Matt Malone heard the distant wail of the ambulance siren heading their way, and he got to his feet. He knew the ambulance had blocks of traffic to get through yet, but he started looking out for it anyway, partly because it kept his eyes from straying back to the two women at his feet. More specifically it kept him from staring at the younger of the two.

He almost felt as if he'd been knocked off his feet like the old woman. He'd never felt such a physical jolt at the sight of a woman as he'd experienced when he'd looked into the face of this dark-haired, blue-eyed stranger. He had an immediate impression of inner strength and a wall of reserve surrounding it. He was good at sizing people up at a glance, but this was something different. This woman attracted him powerfully, almost as if she were daring him to find out what was behind her light blue eyes.

He liked the way she bent protectively over the injured woman. Her thick almost-black hair, cut in a pageboy style, came down nearly to her shoulders, and as she leaned forward it made a dark curtain over her face. But still Matt could see her concern. If I were knocked out in a dark world, he thought, this is who I'd want to have holding my hand.

And yet the only words they'd exchanged had been angry ones.

Matt bent down again beside the two women. "Who is she, do you know?" he asked.

"I don't have any idea."

The blind woman turned her head toward Lily's voice. "Where am I?" she murmured.

"It's all right," Lily said. "You've had an accident. The ambulance is coming for you." Relief, rage and responsibility mingled in her as she looked up toward the noise of the siren and then back to the old woman. All her feelings would be showing on her face, she knew. She'd always been a terrible poker player.

Matt was watching the way her eyes shone. "Why do I get the feeling you're avoiding looking at me?" he asked, bending a little closer to her.

Lily wished he wouldn't. "Because I don't like being stared at," she replied. "Why don't those cars get out of the way and let the ambulance through?"

"Am I staring at you?"

She knew he was, even without staring back. "Yes," she said shortly, "and I can't imagine why."

"What's your name?" This was crazy, Matt knew. The crowd was getting larger, the ambulance was getting closer, but somehow the most important thing was the blue-eyed stranger's name.

She didn't seem to agree. Finally she looked directly at him and Matt was startled all over again by her eyes. They seemed disarmingly open and frank, until he looked a little closer. Then he ran into a polite barrier that made it clear he wasn't welcome. "You need to work on your timing, mister," she told him. "Or do you always make passes at women at the least convenient times?"

Matt was stung. "Back where I come from, asking someone's name isn't counted as making a pass," he said.

"Back where you come from they obviously don't know the rules of the road, either," she said. "If you move that truck of yours, the ambulance can get closer."

"That truck" was a brand new Jeep with all the optional extras, and ordinarily Matt was as careful with it as if it had been his firstborn. But now he pulled it over to the curb in a screeching turn that must have confirmed everything Lily already thought about his driving.

So much for the famous Malone charm, he thought. He was already angry at himself for not being able to stop in time to avoid the blind woman. Now he was fuming at his own awkwardness in dealing with this attractive stranger. She'd been quite right. He'd been pushing her, and the time and place were all wrong. But somehow he hadn't been able to stop himself. The instant he'd seen her, every red blood cell in his body had urged him not to waste any time finding out who she was and what she was all about.

"Coming through!"

Two paramedics pushed through the crowd and knelt beside the semiconscious blind woman. One of them listened to Lily's explanation of what had happened, while the other did a quick examination. To Lily's relief it seemed that there were no serious injuries.

"Cops are on their way," said the first paramedic. "They'll want to talk to you."

Lily stood back out of the way. Her long list of the things she had to do came back to mind, and she looked at her watch, realizing she was going to be much later than she'd hoped getting to Hartford. She looked over at the shining black Jeep, now parked across the street, and caught its driver in the act of looking impatiently at his own watch. Somehow this man did something to her that bothered her profoundly, and she knew it had nothing to do with the accident. The first moment she'd set eyes on him, he'd seemed to encroach on places that she wanted kept very private.

A motorcycle policeman had driven up and was tapping on the Jeep's window. Lily decided she might as well get this over with. She crossed the street and joined the two men.

"I don't want to sound like a hit-and-run," she heard the stranger saying as he stepped onto the sidewalk, "but I'm already late getting to Vermont. Can we make this quick?"

Lily wondered what pressing business was waiting for him. He didn't look like a businessman or anything else that could easily be labeled. Maybe he was a local politician somewhere; that would explain his hurry to get away from an accident. It would explain, too, the easy air of command he had. Whatever his reasons, he was obviously reluctant to stay on the scene.

The policeman was giving him no chance to run off at any speed, Lily was glad to see. "All in good time, sir," he said. "Let's just get some names and addresses to start with."

She glanced at her watch again and sighed. She had wanted to be on the road by dinnertime. This is what I get for trying to be a Good Samaritan, she thought ruefully.

She looked at the old woman, lying helpless and half-conscious on the stretcher, and felt a twinge of regret. If Lily hadn't been so insistent on "helping," no doubt the woman would have bumbled her way across the street in safety.

On the other hand she might have been killed by the first car that came along. At least this way she was still alive and apparently in one piece. Lily would just have to resign herself to the delay.

"Lily Martineau," she said in answer to the policeman's questions. "I'm just in the process of moving to Hartford, Connecticut." She gave the address and phone number of the apartment she'd be sharing with her friend Sarah Bell.

The policeman took down the information as she spoke. Lily was annoyed to find that the auburn-haired stranger had gone back to staring at her. Maybe "staring" wasn't quite the right word—there was an intimacy in his eyes that had no right to be there at all.

"And how did the accident come about?"

"I was trying to help this woman cross the street," Lily said, keeping her eyes on the stranger in front of her. "She seems to have a violent dislike of being touched, but I couldn't think of any other way to point her in the right direction. The light changed and she refused to move, and when I tried to put a hand on her to guide her, she jumped away, right into the next lane of traffic, and this man came speeding along and hit her."

"I hit her," the stranger said distinctly, "because she landed in front of me with absolutely no warning."

"Let's get things in order, sir," the policeman interrupted. "Name?"

"Matt Malone. I live just around the corner, on Beacon Hill." He gave home and office telephone numbers, and Lily wondered again what he did for a living. Wasn't the name Matt Malone vaguely familiar? Lily dug in her memory but couldn't come up with anything.

Malone held her stare the whole time he was speaking to the policeman. This was a problem between the two of them, his dark brown eyes seemed to be saying. Lily held her ground and refused to lower her gaze.

"I was driving along at about thirty miles an hour," he went on, "and I could see these two women arguing in the middle of the street. I suppose I slowed down a little—the traffic was backed up—and then I saw Ms. Martineau put her hand up and push the other woman into my lane."

"I didn't push her!" Lily said hotly. "I put a hand on her to show her the way, and she didn't like it."

"From my point of view, it looked as if she was pushed."

Lily appealed to the policeman. "Why should I push her?" she demanded, turning away from Matt Malone's gaze finally and with difficulty. "If I had, I would have pushed her toward the curb, not away from it."

The policeman refused to take sides. "It's my job to get the evidence," he told them, "not to decide who's right and who's wrong."

Lily pursed her mouth in an angry line. This was official evidence, she knew, and because Matt Malone had misinterpreted what he'd seen, the official evidence could show that Lily had been responsible for the accident.

Well, she wasn't going to take that lying down. "You can add to my evidence," she said to the policeman, "that Mr. Malone seemed to appear out of nowhere. I don't think he could have been going as slowly as he said."

Once again their eyes met, angrier on both sides this time. Matt waited until the policeman had slowly written down Lily's added comment and then said, "If you're done with me, I really am in a hurry. You'll be able to reach me if you need me."

"I'm in a hurry, too," Lily said, "but I think I'll see how the poor woman is doing before I go."

"Better be quick," the policeman told her. "They're about ready to go."

The crowd at the intersection had thinned, and the ambulance was surrounded only by busy people on their lunch hour, hurrying to cross at the light. Lily threaded her way through the throng just as one paramedic was climbing into the back of the vehicle and the other was starting the engine.

"Is she going to be okay?" she asked. It was all very well to argue with Matt Malone about who had caused the accident, but the reality of the frail-looking woman on the stretcher took all the sting out of Lily's anger. When she considered it rationally, Lily knew that the blind woman herself had been the cause of this, but it was impossible to blame her when she looked so helpless.

"She's tough as nails," said the paramedic cheerfully. "Aren't you, Tommy?"

"You know her?"

"Everybody knows her. Tommy's a regular character around here. You'll pull through, won't you?"

The old woman stirred and turned her head toward Lily's voice. "Who hit me?" she demanded, sounding weak but still scrappy.

"A man in a Jeep," Lily said. "The police have his address."

"Good." In spite of her injuries, Tommy's feisty spirit was still very much in evidence. "He'll be hearing from me."

Lily had no doubt of that. She felt a sudden admiration for the elderly woman, coping with a difficult life by standing squarely up to any and all opposition. Perhaps it made her irritable, but at least she was surviving. Lily liked that.

Prompted by this unexpected sympathy, Lily dug into her purse and came up with her business card. Hastily she crossed out her old address and scribbled in the new one in Hartford. "Here," she said, tucking the card into the pocket of Tommy's red dress. "That's my card. If you need advice about the accident, give me a call. I'm a lawyer."

It wasn't until the ambulance had gone that she realized Matt Malone was standing right behind her. He was so close that she was physically aware of the warmth of his body before her mind took in the fact that he hadn't left yet.

"I thought you were in a big hurry to get out of town," she said. She was amazed at the sharpness Matt Malone seemed to bring out in her. He triggered a lot of responses that she didn't expect.

"I was," he admitted. "But I couldn't let you walk away with an exit line like that. I'd have been kicking myself all the way back to Brattleboro if I hadn't even taken two minutes to find out how the patient was doing."

That was a little more like it, Lily thought. But was it real concern, or was he more worried about his image than about the old woman? His good looks and his obvious charm put Lily on her guard. He had too much of both to be trustworthy at first glance. There was something about his rugged build and tousled auburn hair that made her think of the country, and it was unexpectedly appealing. Once again she found herself wondering what he did and why his name rang a bell in her mind.

And then Matt answered her question and killed all her interest in him with one sentence. "Besides," he said, "I didn't realize we were colleagues. I'm a lawyer, too."

Of course. Lily almost said the words out loud. Of course he was a lawyer. It explained his take-charge air, the expensive new Jeep and why his name had been vaguely familiar. It also explained why she'd been subconsciously backpedaling away from his good looks and his hints that he found her attractive.

She was pleased that her instincts had warned her away from Matt even before she'd known he was a lawyer. Mentally she reviewed the rules she'd made for herself. Lawyers as colleagues—fine. Lawyers as friends—okay. But lawyers as lovers were not a possibility for Lily Martineau. Not ever again.

From the look in Matt's eyes, she guessed that he was operating on a different set of rules. It was time to set him straight.

"How interesting," she said. Her voice was cool. "Well, I have a lot of things to do this afternoon, so if you'll excuse me—"

She started to step past him, but he blocked her way. "Wait a minute," he said, sounding puzzled. "The temperature just lowered by about forty degrees. What happened?"

"Nothing happened," she said, looking levelly at him. "And nothing's going to happen. You and I have no further business together, Mr. Malone."

He was frowning now, half-humorously. "I get the feeling I said the wrong thing," he said. "I could swear I just heard a door slam shut somewhere."

"Temperatures dropping, doors slamming—you have quite an imagination," she said.

He grinned. It made him look suddenly boyish. "It's my glib Irish tongue," he said. "It comes in handy in my line of work. *Our* line of work, I should say."

You don't have to remind me, Lily thought. She still couldn't remember just where she'd heard his name, but the fact that she'd heard it at all probably meant that he was well-known and successful in the field. They were the worst, those work-driven lawyers who'd made it to the top.

"I'm sure you're very good at what you do," she countered, "and I don't want to keep you from it any longer. I seem to recall you were in a hurry. Goodbye, Mr. Malone."

This time she sidestepped him neatly and crossed to the other side of the road with a wave of pedestrians. She was careful not to look back, but she was aware, a few seconds later, of the sound of the Jeep's engine starting up and of the vehicle driving off down Tremont Street.

It felt strange to her to be the last one left at the scene of the accident, as though the ambulance and police and Matt's black Jeep had simply vanished into the ether. Lily went over the accident coolly in her mind, making herself concentrate on little details when she found she kept running into a disturbing picture of the look on Matt's handsome face when she'd cut him off. It was a little puzzled, a little frustrated, even a little hurt, perhaps. No matter who or what he was, she didn't like to think that she'd hurt his feelings.

Well, no doubt he'd forget all about her by the time he got to Brattleboro. He looked like a man who wouldn't dwell on his failures. An accident involving an old woman? A mere trifle, not to be allowed to interfere with the more important business of taking lunch with a client.

The thought of lunch made Lily's stomach rumble in a demand for sustenance. It was past one o'clock, and her breakfast had been scanty.

Lunch was likely to be much the same, she thought. There were still too many things to do today, and time was getting short. With an effort she cleared her mind of all thoughts about lawyers and went back to her list of things to do, as she stood on the corner, waiting for the light to change.

TWO

Miraculously things managed to get done. Lily got through a frenzy of last-minute packing, and by five o'clock she was watching the movers take the last box down the three flights of stairs from her apartment to the street. She was finished, she realized with sudden weariness. Now all she had to do was leave.

Somehow that was harder than she'd expected. Was it sentimental attachment for her tiny top-floor abode that was keeping her there sitting on the bare window seat even after she'd heard the moving truck drive away? Surely it couldn't be that. Her place was cozy but far too small, and although she might not be thrilled by her temporary job in Hartford, she *was* looking forward to the big airy apartment she and her friend Sarah were going to share there.

She tried twice to get to her feet, pick up her purse and car keys, and go. On the third try she finally made it, and by then she knew what was bothering her. Lily hated to leave loose ends untied, and the accident this afternoon had created something that she couldn't just walk away from. She knew she wouldn't feel right until she found out how Tommy was, even though it meant delaying her trip a little longer.

She started to reach for the telephone and then remembered that she'd had the service discontinued that day. Well, it would be just as easy to drop by the hospital on her way out of town. Her mind made up, Lily left her apartment keys on the kitchen counter and went down the curved staircase for the last time.

Matt stepped out onto the white marble corridor in the main building at the local college. He was questioning his own sanity and wondering why he thought it would be easy to overlap his old job in Boston with his new law practice in Brattleboro.

Matt felt tired in both body and mind just at the moment. He'd done the hundred-mile commute from Brattleboro to Boston too many times in the past week, and his work in the city had hardly been restful. He'd hoped that his gradual resignation from his law firm there would leave him with less and less to do, but it seemed that all the cases he'd elected to finish up were sticky and demanding.

A call from the college president, telling him there was an emergency and he was needed urgently, had gotten him out of his apartment and into his Jeep before he'd done half the work he'd planned to do today. And in the midst of the usual traffic jam downtown, he'd managed to get himself mixed up in an accident. It hadn't been the most relaxed afternoon.

Once he'd finally gotten to Brattleboro, wondering all the way what disaster had befallen the college—student takeover? faculty strike?—it had been almost a relief to find the problem was simply a legal tangle of words. There had been no real need for panic, but Matt had discovered that when problems arose, people wanted their lawyers there to

hold their hands the same way they wanted their doctors if
they had unexpected pain.

.   Outside the building, he stood for a moment thinking
what a beautiful mid-October day it was. He toyed with the
idea of heading out to the new log house he'd been building
since spring. He could frame in another wall and cook himself some dinner over the fire. The cool, clean air felt good
after the clogged streets of Boston, and he could almost
smell the wood smoke already.

Even as he thought about it, he knew he wouldn't get to
the half-finished cabin tonight. Something was distracting
him, in the form of two light blue eyes and a full, sensuous
mouth.

It was Lily's emphatic parting shot that was sticking in
Matt's memory so persistently. She'd said goodbye with all
the firmness of a bouncer showing an unwanted customer
to the door, and he could still see the look in those eyes as
she'd said it. *Don't bother arguing,* her expression had said.

But Matt Malone lived by arguing. He thrived on it, and
he was very good at it. Lily had obviously written him off
for some unfathomable reason. He couldn't explain why
one brief encounter should make him want to prove so desperately to her that she was wrong about him, but that was
exactly what was happening.

Could it be that with his first look at Lily Martineau,
Matt had found himself so intrigued that for the rest of the
afternoon she'd never really left his mind? He knew his
chances of finding her again were slim, but he didn't seem
to be able to do anything except think about her. With one
regretful thought for the lovely evening he'd be missing in
Vermont, Matt climbed into his Jeep and started the two-
hour drive back to Boston.

Lily leaned her head against the lounge wall and listened
to the hospital noises around her—phones ringing, feet tap-
tapping on the polished floors. All the subdued hustle and
bustle was making her feel even more tired.

The hospital was a big one, and it had taken Lily some time just to find where they'd taken Tommy after the emergency room. Finally she'd found the right wing and floor. Tommy's attending doctor, a resident, was busy with someone else, and Lily had been told she'd have to wait to speak with him.

She had decided to wait, since she was delayed anyway. She knew the drive to Hartford would seem even longer if she was wondering the whole way how the old woman was faring.

She closed her eyes, wishing she could cultivate the ability to take catnaps. Even a quick rest would have been welcome at the moment. Then she opened her eyes rather abruptly because the first image that flashed into her mind was that of Matt Malone. She could picture the look in his brown eyes so clearly—part antagonism and part amusement, as though he relished a good argument.

Well, that stood to reason. Most lawyers were mighty arguers by nature. But there had been something else in Matt's eyes that Lily didn't quite understand. It had reached out to her and taken hold, and for some reason it reminded her powerfully of desire.

She told herself she was lucky not to have to deal with Matt Malone on a regular basis. He was too attractive for her safety. She made herself conjure up the memory of Alexander, who was also a handsome man and a lawyer. If she needed anything else to quench the attraction she felt for Matt Malone, the thought of her broken engagement and the accompanying pain was enough to do it.

"Dr. Aiello to reception please. Dr. Aiello to reception."

Lily's eyes opened with a start. She must have been catnapping after all. Certainly she'd lost track of where she was for the past fifteen minutes. I'd better get some coffee, she thought, or I'll never stay awake all the way to Hartford.

She reached for her purse and stood up, stretching her tired muscles. At least now she wasn't feeling quite so grubby; the last item on her list before leaving her apart-

ment had been to take a shower and change her clothes, so
the baggy sweatshirt and faded jeans had been replaced by
a lightweight pair of black pants and a bright red cotton
sweater.

Lily had noticed a coffee machine just around the corner, and she headed for it now. She hadn't gone ten steps
before she ran right into Matt Malone.

There wasn't an actual collision this time, but both of
them stopped so suddenly that they might as well have hit
something. Lily opened her mouth to speak and then closed
it again. She was caught completely off guard not only by
Matt's presence but by the sudden realization that she was
glad to see him again.

The instant Matt laid eyes on Lily, he knew that it had
been more than worth it battling the Friday rush-hour traffic
to find her. He smiled at her. "I thought you'd be halfway
to Connecticut by now," he said.

"And I thought you'd be in Vermont," she returned,
thinking that the quirky grin suited his handsome face.

"I was," he said. "I've been there and back already."

That stopped her for an instant. She'd been picturing him
as just another career-oriented lawyer whose work was near-
sacred. "I assume you had to come back anyway," she said,
making the words into a question.

He raised his eyebrows, and the grin went away, "Maybe
I came back to see how our friend was doing," he said. "Do
you always assume the worst about people you hardly
know?"

"I do know that you seemed in an awful hurry to get away
earlier this afternoon," Lily countered. "What changed
your mind?"

You did, he almost answered and then stopped himself.
"I've always been quick to fire up," he said, "and quick to
cool down again. It occurred to me that I was a bit hasty
about things earlier."

Lily smiled at him, her blue eyes lighting up with amusement. "'Hasty' was one word that came to mind," she said,

and was pleased to see an answering smile on his face. She liked the sense of rugged honesty that she felt from him.

"I don't think I want to hear the other words," he said. "I really did have to be at an important conference, if that's any consolation, but I came back right after it."

Lily's smile faded. The jury was still out on him, she reminded herself. He was probably just as much of a workaholic as the rest of the lawyers she knew. She was glad he was concerned for Tommy's welfare, but he'd still put it in second place, after his important conference.

"Better late than not at all," she said lightly. "The doctor should be here soon. Want a cup of coffee while we wait?"

They drank their coffee in near silence. Lily thought Matt seemed strangely disinterested in Tommy's condition in spite of the concern he'd expressed. Was he regretting the impulse that had brought him back?

A worse thought occurred to her. The man was a lawyer, after all, and in the ambulance Tommy had said that Matt would be hearing from her. To a lawyer, that would mean only one thing: a lawsuit. Had Matt come back to see how things stood and to do what he could to guard himself against a suit?

Lily looked warily at him, trying to read what was on his mind. He looked thoughtful enough, but his strong face and dark eyes weren't giving away any secrets. There was something very sensuous about his lips, she thought—something that hinted of force mingled with gentleness.

He caught her eye almost as if he'd heard her thoughts, and Lily felt her cheeks redden slightly. Then they were both distracted by the welcome appearance of Tommy's doctor.

"Three cracked ribs" was his brusque pronouncement, "and some bruising from the fall. Nothing life-threatening. She'll be in bed for a while. It takes longer to mend when you're getting old, and Tommy's no spring chicken."

"You sound as though this has happened to her before," Lily said. There was something about the doctor's manner that suggested a parent patiently bandaging a child's knee for the umpteenth time.

"Oh, she's an old friend around here," he replied. "She's as stubborn as they come, and it's always getting her into trouble. Are you the young lady who was involved in the accident?"

"Yes. And this is the gentleman who hit her," she added pointedly, looking at Matt.

"Well, if it makes you folks feel any better, you're not the first people Tommy Thompson's involved in accidents like this. She wanders around looking helpless and lost, and people try to help her out, and—well, I guess I don't need to tell you what happens."

"You certainly don't," Lily said with feeling.

"Could she deal with a couple of visitors?" Matt asked, and once again Lily wondered if he was here simply to try to avoid a lawsuit.

"Afraid not." The doctor yawned. "Pardon me. It's the end of the shift, and I'm beat. No, Tommy's under sedation at the moment. I don't think she'll have visitors until tomorrow."

"Well, that settles that." Matt sounded almost relieved.

The doctor yawned once more, then left them.

On their way out through the main entrance, Lily and Matt passed the gift shop, and Lily said impulsively, "I think I'd like to send some flowers up to her room."

"Flowers, for a blind person?" Matt sounded doubtful.

Lily smiled ruefully. "I know," she said, "but I want to do something since we can't visit her. I'll get her roses; that way she can smell them, at least."

She ordered a half-dozen long-stemmed red roses. "Make it a dozen, and I'll pay for half of them," Matt intervened. "It's only fair; it's half my accident, too, after all."

That was a change from his claiming complete innocence and trying to shove the blame onto her, Lily thought. She was more relieved than she'd showed at the doctor's words. In the back of her mind there had been a nagging feeling of guilt about Tommy's injuries, and it was good to know that the doctor placed the blame squarely on Tommy's own shoulders.

Lily and Matt wrote out the card together while the sales clerk made their bouquet in the back room. Lily printed the words "Best wishes for a speedy recovery," wishing it didn't sound so hackneyed, and then both of them signed their names. They were standing close together at the counter, and Lily was already having a hard enough time fighting down her physical response to Matt's nearness when he broke the silence by saying, "Whatever that perfume is you're wearing, it's driving me crazy."

She turned toward him and found herself under a very direct gaze. "I'm not wearing perfume," she said, hearing the slight breathlessness in her voice. "I just had a shower before I left my old apartment—maybe it's the shampoo you're smelling."

She liked the way his smile started in his eyes and then slowly turned his mouth into that quirky grin. "I've smelled a lot of shampoo in my time, lady," he informed her, "and no matter what the ads may try to tell me, I never came across any that got me all hot and bothered. But this—" He leaned forward suddenly, and before Lily could react, he had buried his handsome face in the thick hair around her neck, not kissing her, but letting the warm embrace of his breath surround her as though he wanted to find out the very essence of her.

It was crazy to be this drawn to a stranger, Lily knew, but she was having the hardest time resisting the urge to raise her hands to his broad chest. He must know how she was responding to him. Her own pulse rang in her ears, drowning out all other sounds.

When he slowly raised his head, he was still smiling. "As I suspected," he said, his voice low, "it has nothing to do with shampoo. It's pure Lily Martineau, and it makes me want to know a whole lot more about you than I do now."

Careful, Lily, she warned herself silently. An attraction
this strong could be a very dangerous thing. It could make
her forget her painfully learned lesson about mixing lawyers and love.

"Well, I guess this is better than making a pass at me in
the middle of an accident," she said shakily, trying to laugh.
"But I'm afraid it's still not going to get you any farther,
Mr. Malone. I'm already very late getting out of the city,
and—"

He overrode her words with the air of someone who is
used to dealing with objections. "You can't be thinking of
driving all the way to Hartford on an empty stomach," he
said. "Come and have dinner with me first."

"It's only a two-hour drive," she pointed out.

"It's not good to drive on an empty stomach," he said so
insistently that she had to laugh.

"That's one I never heard before," she said. "Do you
always have this much trouble taking no for an answer?"

"Yes, when I really want something," he growled. "And
I really want to have dinner with you, Lily." Matt was having a great deal of difficulty not reaching out and taking her
in his arms and kissing her until that distantly polite look left
her face. How could a woman seem so gentle and so resili-
ent at the same time? Even her soft voice seemed to hint at
a hidden inner core of strength. And beneath that—what?

"Anyway, we deserve a celebration now that we've made
sure we're not a couple of murderers," he went on. "And I
should warn you, I'm very good at talking people into
things, so you'll save us both a lot of time if you just agree
right now."

Lily had always hated being bullied into anything, but her
objections to Matt fizzled to nothing when she saw the look
on his face. It was eager, hopeful, persuasive—and it mirrored everything she'd been feeling since she'd run into him
in the hospital corridor an hour ago.

She didn't have time for dinner, she knew. It wasn't fair
to expect Sarah to deal with the movers alone, and she

wanted to get a few boxes unpacked before she fell into bed tonight. There was only one possible answer to Matt's invitation.

"All right," she said. "I'd love to have dinner with you."

Three

Half an hour later, Lily was taking the menu the waiter handed her and bracing herself for the inevitable round of invariable questions. "Where did you go to law school? Does Professor So-and so still teach contract law there? Who did you clerk for last year?" Lily had never met a lawyer who didn't start immediately with shoptalk.

But Matt astonished her by saying, "I have to tell you that you have the most beautiful blue eyes I've ever seen."

He took her so completely by surprise that Lily had to laugh. "I'm afraid I can't take the credit for them," she said. "They're Martineau eyes, according to my father."

"Are his the same color?"

"They were. He died when I was small."

"How did he die?"

Matt's question was so gentle that it seemed natural for Lily to answer it without stopping to think that she very rarely told anyone, even friends, about her family. "He and my mother were on a car trip across the country. I'd been spending the summer with my aunt and uncle in California, and they were driving from New York to pick me up and take me home. A truck went out of control and hit them. They were both killed instantaneously.''

Matt's face was suddenly more serious, and he brushed the back of her hand briefly with his fingertips. ''That must have been tough,'' he said.

''It was. I was nine at the time, old enough to feel responsible for the whole thing. If they hadn't been coming to get me, they wouldn't have been killed.''

''I hope you got over that feeling,'' he said soberly.

''I did, but it took a long time.'' She shook her thick dark hair back from her face, and Matt was left with the sneaking suspicion that deep down, Lily had never quite recovered from the sudden loss of both parents.

''Where did you live after that?'' he asked.

''I stayed with my aunt and uncle in California.''

''Somehow I get the feeling you weren't thrilled about it,'' he said when she paused.

''What is this, a cross-examination?''

''Sorry. Just a habit, I guess.''

''I can tell. You must be very good in the courtroom. What firm do you work for, anyway?''

Matt frowned. She'd neatly deflected the subject of her family, he noticed. Clearly it wasn't something she liked talking about. He debated rephrasing his question and trying again, and decided to wait.

''Sloan and Baker,'' he said, naming one of Boston's oldest and most respected firms.

Lily's eyes opened wider and then became thoughtful. ''I thought your name sounded familiar,'' she said, ''but I couldn't put it in context. Didn't you handle that big bank merger for them last spring?'' She remembered the case clearly. It had been a hostile takeover of a small bank by a larger one, and it had gotten a great deal of publicity. Sloan and Baker, she recalled, had engineered things for the winning side.

"I did." Matt was watching Lily very closely, and her re-action was puzzling him. After her recognition that he was Sloan and Baker's star attorney, he could have sworn he saw something in her face that looked like disapproval. It didn't make any sense.

"I seem to end up with all the high-profile cases," he said with a self-deprecating smile. "Sometimes I envy the law-yers I know who have a quieter time with things."

"Somehow I don't believe you," she replied. "You have quite a reputation, as I'm sure you know."

"A reputation as what?"

She looked him straight in the eye. "As an ambitious lawyer who loves a fight," she said.

"Something wrong with that?"

"Nothing at all." *Except that you're exactly the kind of man I try to steer clear of,* Lily added silently. She pushed her hair back again. It always acted up just after she'd washed it.

Matt followed the gesture with his eyes. His desire to touch her was so strong that he could almost feel his fin-gers tangling themselves in those thick dark tresses. He had to take a deep breath before he could get himself back to a purely conversational level.

The Italian restaurant they'd chosen was a small one, and the tables were so close together that there wasn't the sense of privacy that Matt had wished for. But because the noise level was high, Lily and Matt had to lean toward each other over their small table to make themselves heard, and he didn't object to that at all.

"So you're going to Hartford to take a job?" he asked.

"A temporary one. A friend of mine is working as legal counsel for an insurance company there, and they need someone to do a legal survey for them for the next few months." She tried to make herself look interested.

Matt picked up on that immediately. "I'm not seeing a sparkle of enthusiasm in those pretty blue eyes," he com-mented with a smile.

"Is it that obvious?" She smiled back in spite of herself.
"My friend Sarah is convinced it's a great career, but it's
just not the kind of law I'm interested in. It *is* a job though,
and nobody else was knocking on my door."

The waiter arrived to take their order, and Lily was glad
of the interruption. She reminded herself firmly that this
was nothing more than a quick dinner with a friendly man.
True, when she looked into the friendly man's eyes she felt
a flutter of excitement that startled her every time it happened. But just because she was physically attracted didn't
mean she was deaf to common sense.

Matt was a lawyer. A very successful, high-powered lawyer, and she knew what that meant. Work came first. It had
to, since he'd made it to the top of his profession. And that
left no time for a home life or a family or a romance, or any
of the things that were important to Lily.

She hadn't always been so adamant about these things,
but her recent experience had left her wiser if sadder.

After the waiter had gone, Matt returned to the subject of
Lily's family. "So I get the impression you're an only
child," he said.

Lily recognized that she was dealing with world-class
persistence in Matt Malone. But she'd already told him more
than he needed to know, and she deflected his implied
question by turning it into a joke.

"My mother always said that when she discovered her
first child was so nice and well-mannered, she decided she'd
better not push her luck by trying to have another," she said.
"She was fond of having things neat and orderly."

"And you take after her."

"How do you mean?"

"There's something about you that seems to want things
to be...correct. Even this afternoon, in the middle of that
accident, you were just as calm as you are now."

She certainly didn't feel calm. There was a constant sensation of excitement inside her, and try as she might to
blame it on the eventful day she'd had, she knew it was

simply the closeness of Matt Malone that was making her react that way.

But she knew what he meant. She'd always had that wall of reserve around her, and she was aware that it put some people off. "I've always been that way," she told Matt. "Does it bother you?"

He considered the question for a moment, and when he answered, there was a glint of more than just amusement in his eyes. "Let's say I find it something of a challenge," he said. "It makes me want to find out what's going on beneath it."

"You might find that more difficult than you think." Lily's heart rate was accelerating, giving the lie to her words. She was managing to keep her poise—but only barely.

"Maybe," Matt said, "but maybe not. You're working pretty hard on that image of yours, Lily Martineau, but if I really put my mind to it, I know I could shake you up."

There was no missing the meaning of his words. His smile had become positively sensual, and there was a look of satisfaction in his eyes that seemed to say, "See? I'm doing it already." Lily had thought she'd been successful in hiding the effect this handsome man had on her, and it was disturbing to find out that he was not only aware of it, but already one jump ahead of her.

One jump to where? This encounter couldn't possibly lead them anywhere. After dinner, they'd go back to their separate lives and careers. And that was the way Lily wanted it. If she gave way to his charm, she might find herself halfway down a road she'd promised she wouldn't travel again.

She decided she'd better get the conversation back on a safer track, and fast. "You know," she said as though she'd misunderstood the hidden meanings in Matt's last words, "you're a surprising man. Here we are, two lawyers sitting down to dinner, and all you've done is ask me questions about myself. You should be talking about the latest Supreme Court ruling, or complaining about the latest client your firm saddled you with. I'm beginning to wonder if you really *are* a lawyer after all."

Annoyingly he seemed to know the reason why she'd changed the subject. All right, those perceptive eyes told her, we'll get back to it soon enough.

"Oh, I'm a bona fide lawyer, all right," he said, "but in my book it's a crime to have dinner with a beautiful woman and do nothing but talk shop."

Lily couldn't keep her surprise out of her voice. "Now I'm *sure* you're not a lawyer," she said. "Lawyers are physically incapable of not talking shop."

"What about you?" he asked reasonably. "You asked me about my firm, after all."

He was right, and Lily frowned. Normally she was so careful to keep the law and her social life from overlapping. "That doesn't count as shoptalk," she hedged. "It was just simple curiosity. I was trying to find out where I knew your name from."

"Not the strongest of arguments, but we'll give you points for coming up with it in a hurry," he said.

Lily's frown deepened. His tone made her think of a schoolmaster grading a student's performance, and she resented it. Once again she sidestepped the issue and changed the subject.

"Sometimes I think I'm the only living specimen of a lawyer who thinks there are other things in life besides the law," Lily said.

Matt smiled. "I have to admit," he said, "that I can be as single-minded as anyone about my work, but lately I've had a sneaking suspicion that there might be other things in life that are worthwhile, too."

"That's heresy, you know," Lily informed him.

His smile turned into a laugh. It was a sound that was easy to get caught up in. "We're an endangered species," he said, "but there are a few of us out there. Welcome to the club."

He held out his right hand, and Lily hesitated for just a moment before she reached out to shake it. He was still calling the shots—she would swear he'd initiated the handshake simply for them to have an excuse to touch.

But her reservations vanished instantly as she realized how good his touch felt. Matt's hand was big and strong, like the rest of him. Lily would have been more than happy to let her hand rest in his, and her imagination treacherously continued on from there. She couldn't keep from thinking how it would feel to be curled in Matt's embrace, with those arms around her.

Regretfully, she made herself stop. "What about you?" she asked, reclaiming her hand. "What's your pedigree?"

"Pure Boston Irish," he said, keeping his hand on the linen tablecloth as though he hoped he might have a chance to recapture hers at any moment. "I'm an only child, too, but for a slightly different reason. I think when my parents found out what a holy terror I was, they decided not to have any more."

"And what makes a holy terror decide to be a lawyer?"

"I love a good fight, as you've already pointed out." There was mischief in Matt's eyes.

Lily knew several lawyers who had gone into law simply because they enjoyed arguing about things, and she'd found them all tiresome after a very short while. But Matt Malone didn't seem to fall into that category—or any other category, as far as she could tell—and she wanted to know more.

"Don't you think the law deserves a more serious attitude than that?" she asked him.

There it was again, Matt thought, that polite, almost standoffish air she had. He forced his attention back to her words and away from the overpowering need he felt to soften her expression into something like passion.

"Oh, I'm serious enough about it," he replied. "But I have to admit I enjoy it, too. I like being with people, and I get a kick out of solving problems. I don't see why you can't be serious about something and have fun with it at the same time."

"I suppose I've always tended to separate the two things," Lily said thoughtfully.

"Of course you have. I can see it written all over your face. But you just wait till you've had some courtroom experience; you'll find out what I mean about loving a good fight."

"What makes you think I don't have any courtroom experience?" Was that written all over her face, too? And here she thought she'd been giving one of her most sterling performances as Lily Martineau, poised and worldly attorney-at-law.

"Just a guess," he said. "There's something slightly tentative about you, and I'm presuming it comes from inexperience. And having a great detective brain, as well as as a good legal one, I deduce that you're not long out of school, just passed the bar, and are now about to launch your career on an unsuspecting world."

He was far too pleased with himself about his sleuthing, she thought. And the annoying thing was that he was right in every particular.

It was time to reassert herself, she thought. "Are you always such a whirlwind," she demanded, "or is this a special effort?"

He disconcerted her by leaning even closer over the little table. There was still mischief dancing in those brown eyes, and a strong hint of something else. "I'm *almost* always such a whirlwind," he answered, and left his words unexplained. But his meaning was only too clear.

"Now—" he leaned back again "—tell me more. What are you planning to do after your less-than-fascinating temporary job in Hartford?"

"I knew we'd get around to shoptalk." Lily wondered if her heartbeat was ever going to slow down. She was half-entranced just by his voice. It was rich and warm and managed to sound amused and amorous all at once.

"It's not talk about shop," he said simply. "It's talk about you. Now tell me. What made you decide to be a lawyer?"

And then, because it seemed very easy to tell things to Matt Malone, Lily found herself explaining how she'd decided at fifteen on a legal career and how the order and objectivity of the legal system had always appealed to her.

"What a nice, romantic view of the law," he said, gently poking fun.

His eyes were smiling so invitingly that Lily couldn't take offense at his words. "I suppose you're right," she said, "and I know I'm inexperienced and all that. But I still believe the law is there to straighten out problems and determine what's right. If I didn't believe that, I would have gone into some other field."

"Such as?"

She looked up, suddenly shy. "I don't know," she hedged. "I've always been fond of art. Painting, I mean. I don't have what it takes to be a great artist, but I suppose if I weren't a lawyer, I'd have a try at it."

"Do you paint now?"

"Sometimes." Lily felt as if he'd just seen her unclothed, and the thought was so seductive that she found herself blushing. Her paintings were something intensely private, completely her own. Very few people knew about them. How had Matt Malone managed to become one of them, and on such short notice?

"Anyway," she said firmly, "I'm not a painter, I'm a lawyer, and eventually I'm hoping to find a firm where I feel I'm actually helping people, instead of just making money."

"I think every law student has that idea at first," Matt said. His tone was neutral. Was he scornful or approving?

Law student. Lily felt like a teenager again. Matt had years of experience on important cases under his belt. Who was she to start lecturing him about the meaning of the law?

"I guess that seems pretty naive," she said, keeping her own voice neutral.

"Not at all. It's a worthwhile goal if you can manage to achieve it. Sometimes it demands a huge slice of your life if you really get involved in it."

"Well, it's not going to demand a huge slice of mine," Lily said promptly. "I'm not going to be one of those lawyers who doesn't know where work ends and real life begins."

Matt raised an eyebrow at her. "Somehow I sense something behind that remark," he said.

She hadn't meant to sound so challenging, but now that she'd approached the awkward subject, she might as well follow through. "How many hours a week do you work?" she asked him.

"Oh, Lord." Matt drew a strong hand across his face. "For the past few years, it's seemed like all of them."

"That's exactly what I *don't* intend to do," she said. "And if I do give up some of my private life for work, it's got to be something that's pretty darn important to me."

"Implying that my work isn't?"

"I don't know. Is it?"

She wasn't usually this bold even with people she'd known for years. She had a ridiculous little hope that Matt might be too good to be true—a lawyer who worked for ideals he believed in. But she knew it was a long shot. Besides, he'd already admitted he spent more time working than not. That was one of the biggest danger signals.

· He took a long time in answering, as though he was trying to make up his mind how honest to be. Finally he said, "I have to admit that none of my work at Sloan and Baker comes under the category of 'helping people out,' as you phrased it. We do mostly corporate law, which is pretty dry stuff."

"But pays well." What was one more challenge while she was at it?

"Disgustingly well." He raised an eyebrow at her. "I suppose that labels me as a sellout."

"I'm not in the habit of labeling people," she told him. "But it's fairly clear that we have very different ideas about the law, Mr. Malone."

And about the rest of life, too, she almost added. It was too bad. Matt was an intelligent, very attractive man, but he was the last man in the world for Lily Martineau.

Matt could sense her cooling down, and he wondered what was behind her obvious disapproval of him. Clearly she wanted nothing to do with lawyers who put in long hours for high pay, working on cases that didn't interest them personally. Which was curious, he thought, because that included a large percentage of the profession, as Lily must know.

He didn't like the polite, distant look that had come back to her face. A couple of times during dinner, she'd smiled wholeheartedly at him, and he'd caught a glimpse of a dimple in her cheek that had suddenly transformed her face and given a hint of what lay beneath that keep-your-distance expression. He wanted to tease that dimple out again and make it stay.

He might be able to do that by telling her the whole story of his slow resignation from Sloan and Baker, and his decision to start a practice on his own in Brattleboro. But he knew he shouldn't spill those beans just yet; Derek Sloan had asked him to keep his decision quiet until he'd wound up a couple of important cases. He owed a lot to Sloan, and he'd promised to be discreet about leaving the firm.

Well, then, he'd just have to try something else to make Lily Martineau smile at him again. He leaned forward with a mock frown on his face and said in his best Malone-for-the-defense voice, "Enough small talk, lady. Let's talk about us. I'm assuming you're not married."

He made the sentence into a question, trying to sound lighthearted. But he immediately knew he'd said the wrong thing. Lily's face clouded, and she glanced at her hands. Matt followed her gaze. She wore no rings, but something in her eyes made Matt think that maybe she had. Until recently, perhaps? He kicked himself for being so flippant about it.

"No, I'm not married," she said levelly.

Matt reached across the table and put both his hands over hers. "I realize it's not really any of my business," he said, "but I have a good reason for asking."

"And what's your good reason?" His touch felt so good, Lily thought. She had to resist the powerful impulse to turn her hands palms up and grasp his tightly.

"I find you very, very attractive," he began seriously enough, and then a grin broke through. "Hell, that's too tame a way to put it. It makes my blood race just to look at you, Lily. I want to see you again, soon. And I just want to make sure you're not involved with anyone else."

When she'd broken her engagement to Alexander early this summer, Lily had been sure it would take her a long time to get close to anyone again. Which had been fine by her—she'd had enough heartache for the next half-dozen years. But somehow Matt Malone must have come to mean something to her since today at noon, because she was amazed at how much it hurt to turn him down. Without really meaning to, she intertwined her fingers with his.

"I'm not involved with anyone else," she said, "but that doesn't mean I'm planning to get involved with you, either. I may not have much experience as a lawyer, Matt, but there is one thing I know for certain. I keep my home life and my work life strictly separate. And that means no romance with lawyers."

"That's ridiculous," Matt said bluntly. "That's like saying no romance with brown-eyed men, or with men who like seafood. All lawyers aren't the same, Lily."

Lily's chin tilted up, and she pulled her hands from his grasp. "A lot of them are, and I dare you to deny it," she said. "The vast majority of the lawyers I know put their careers first, which means working long, long hours and never really being away from the job, even when they're at home."

Matt started to argue out of habit and then stopped. He'd already admitted to his own long work hours, so he couldn't contradict her statement. "There's nothing wrong with being involved in your job," he said instead, surprised at how defensive he sounded.

"Nothing at all. It just happens that the next time I get involved with a man, I want someone who's home for dinner more than one night a week, and who'll actually go on vacation without taking a truckload of work along."

The next time. She sounded as though she was speaking from experience. Matt filed that thought away for future reference.

"I'm not saying that lawyers shouldn't work eighty hours a week," Lily continued. "I'm just saying that that doesn't fit in with my idea of what a relationship should be."

"What if you found a lawyer who worked forty hours a week and never brought his work home?" Matt demanded.

"I'd suspect he was pulling my leg," she said. "And if he wasn't, then maybe I'd consider it. But I hope you're not trying to convince me you fall into that category."

"I guess there isn't much chance of that, is there? I'm intrigued, though. Tell me more about your idea of what a relationship should be," he said.

"I think two people should share things right down the middle," she said. "That means decisions, chores, family—"

"You want a family of your own?"

She stiffened a little at that, as though he were digging too deeply. But he'd kept his voice carefully casual, and finally she seemed to decide it was all right to tell him.

"Yes," she said almost defiantly. "I lost the one I had when I was nine years old. My parents and I were always good buddies while they were alive, and I guess I miss it. My aunt and uncle had four kids, but I never felt like part of that family."

"Didn't they treat you well?"

"Oh, it was nothing like that. It was just—I felt like a fifth wheel. I don't think they intentionally put me in last place. I suppose it's natural to love your own children more than one you...inherited." There was a touch of bitterness in her voice no matter how hard she tried to keep it out. She knew some of the bitterness was because of Alexander. She'd thought until this summer that she'd finally found a person she came first with, only to discover that for Alexander the law came first, and love—and she—a distant second. But she wasn't going to explain everything to Matt Malone. She finished up brusquely. "So, yes, it's very important to me to have children someday and try to make a family life for myself again."

When he didn't say anything right away, she added, "So you can imagine that what I want out of a relationship can't possibly include a man who's already married to his job."

That phrase sounded as though she'd already said it to someone else, Matt thought, and decided to play his hunch. "You sound very sure about all this," he said. "What happened to make you so dead set against romance with lawyers?"

He thought he could guess, but he wanted to see if she would tell him. Apparently she wouldn't.

"Nothing happened," she replied. "I'm just using my own common sense, that's all. And my common sense tells me that although you're a very attractive man, Matt, and I like you a lot, we'd be smarter just to call it quits right now before anything happens. And speaking of calling it quits, I really should get out of here. I'd completely lost track of the time."

Maybe *you* think nothing's happened yet, Matt thought grimly as they paid the bill and left the restaurant. He felt as if he were a different person from the Matt Malone who'd raced out of his apartment that afternoon. Meeting Lily had opened up a whole new world of possibilities for him.

And now she was politely but firmly closing that door in his face. He walked with her to her car, grappling with the knowledge that she was about to drive away and out of his life. He was trying to rally his well-known persuasiveness to talk her into agreeing to see him again, but somehow he could think of nothing but the need to hold her just once. Maybe that was better than words anyway. Maybe if he forced her to admit to the magnetic pull he knew was between them, she'd soften her stance. And besides, he couldn't stand to find her and lose her in a single day without even a taste of her lips.

He held out against his growing desire until Lily was on the very point of getting into her car, and then, in a voice that was almost a growl, he said, "You're still sure we're not going to see each other again?"

"I don't see why we would," she said firmly, "unless I happen to be standing in the middle of an intersection some day and you come speeding along again."

It was her expression that finally drove him over the edge. She'd reverted once again to the slightly distant look, the one that said, "Lily Martineau is private property, not to be entered without permission." It wasn't just the wide-openness of those light blue eyes, or the slight upward tilt of her small chin. It was the challenge he felt in his bones, to break down that wall of reserve and *make* her respond to him.

She'd gotten as far as reaching for the door handle when she was arrested by the look on Matt's face. And there wasn't time to react to it before he captured her in his arms and she was suddenly surrounded by the warm, breathing strength of him.

"Lily..." He spoke her name with his lips against her hair. She knew this was a mistake, but the slight masculine scent of Matt's skin was driving her wild. Deep inside her, she could feel a pulsating answer to the question in Matt's voice.

The strength of his kiss took her by surprise. She could sense the built-up reserves of desire in him as she lost herself in pure sensation. The fury of his embrace gave way t

a tender exploration, and the whole world around them—
the quiet gas-lit side street where Lily had parked, the late-
summer balminess of the city air—dwindled to the place
where they stood, locked together as though they were
fighting against the time when they would have to separate.

Matt's lips covered hers so persuasively, moving gently
until she couldn't help but respond to him. Then the warmth
of his tongue filled her mouth, and she was amazed at her
own boldness as she entwined her tongue with his and invited him to an even more intimate embrace.

He tasted faintly of the red wine he'd had at dinner, but
there was more to it than that. Lily returned his kisses with
growing hunger, trying to capture the rich, warm flavor—or
was it a scent—that acted on nerve endings deep inside her
body. Her hands were lost in the thickness of his russet hair,
and the sounds of desire from deep in his throat were as in-
toxicating to her as any drug.

"Beep-beep-beep-beep-beep!"

Lily's eyes flew open, and the soft darkness she'd been
seeing behind her closed lids vanished. The piercing sound
was coming from right next to her ear, and after a second or
two she recognized it as a beeper, lodged in Matt's jacket
pocket and insistently reminding both of them that he was
a lawyer who was much in demand and that someone was
demanding him right now.

"Damn!" Matt reached into his pocket and shut the
beeper off, but by then Lily's guard was up higher than ever,
and when he tried to recapture her in his arms, she slipped
away and made it to the safe ground of the driver's seat.

Matt leaned against the car, keeping the door open. Lily's
cheeks were almost as red as her sweater, he noticed, as if
she were astonished at her own response to his kiss. Or
maybe she was just angry at the interruption.

"I don't usually wear one of these things," he said. He
was trying to speak gently, but she'd turned the key in the
ignition, and he had to raise his voice to make himself heard

over the engine's noise. "It's just that I'm in the middle of a big case right now, and—"

"Please don't make excuses, Matt," she said. "I've heard them all, and they don't make things any better."

He *had* to know what made her feel this way. "Lily, you've been hurt by someone, haven't you? Another lawyer?"

Slam! The door closed, sounding like an iron cage to Matt's ears. Lily rolled down the window two inches. "I told you," she said. "It's just common sense."

He was starting to feel angry now. She really was going to vanish on him just as she'd threatened. "I hope you find your common sense keeps you company," he said, "because you could wait a long time for that perfect man you're planning on."

"I know what I want, and I'm willing to wait until I find it," she informed him. "And my common sense is a lot better company than a beeper that won't let me forget my job for a minute."

And with that, she was gone, and the glib Matt Malone, famous in certain circles for never losing an argument, was left without even getting in the last word. He stood there for a long time after she'd left, and then reluctantly headed for a phone booth to put in a call to his answering service. He had a momentary urge to hike the other way and throw the damn beeper into the Charles River, but his sense of duty was just too strong.

He wondered, as he dug in his pockets for change, how he could have imagined that one kiss would satisfy the ache he felt inside at the thought of Lily Martineau. He knew this feeling wouldn't leave until he held Lily in his arms again.

There was one thing he felt completely satisfied about. In the instant just after she'd pulled back and before she'd realized what the beeping noise was, he'd seen that the look of distant politeness had vanished from her face. She'd been open and warm and responsive, all the things he'd sensed were hidden inside her. He might never see her again—that thought cost him a pang—but he suspected he'd reached a part of Lily that no one else knew was there.

It took only three days before Lily found out that she would be seeing Matt again.

She'd wondered a thousand times just what had gone on between them, and had replayed their dinnertime conversation over and over in her mind. She'd pictured a hundred and fifty different ways that they might see each other again, all involving circumstances that seemed very unlikely ever to happen.

The reality was something she'd never even considered. One day in the mail she received a letter from a law firm in Boston. Instead of being a job offer, as she'd hoped, it was a letter stating that Thomasina Thompson held both Lily Martineau and Matthew Malone responsible for physical and mental suffering caused by them jointly, and that unless they paid her a substantial amount in damages, she had every intention of taking them both to court.

Four

"Sloan and Baker. May I help you?"

Even the secretary at Sloan and Baker sounded as though she had important business waiting for her, Lily thought. She could picture the old building in downtown where the law firm had been for over a hundred years. Lily had never been inside, but the building had always given her the impression of old-fashioned decor and lots of dark oak paneling. It was hard to picture Matt, with his vigorous, outdoorsy air, in that atmosphere.

"Matthew Malone, please," Lily said. It had been two days since the letter had appeared, and she'd decided it was time to see what Matt had to say about it.

"I'm sorry," the secretary replied, "but he's in an important conference at the moment, and he can't be interrupted. May I take a message?"

Lily's heart sank a little. Of course he would be in an important conference. He was, after all, a much sought-after man.

When she'd finally arrived in Hartford that night five days ago, she'd apologetically told Sarah about the accident and had mentioned Matt by name rather casually. Sarah had whistled, impressed.

"You'd better hope he doesn't decide to sue you," she'd commented. "He's got a reputation for being able to talk anybody into anything. He'd probably have you admitting you were at fault, and happily paying damages before you knew what had happened."

"Somehow I don't think he's going to sue," Lily had replied, never dreaming that she and Matt would both be sued.

She realized that Matt's secretary was waiting for an answer, and reluctantly she acknowledged the fact that Matt wasn't someone she could call up and talk to whenever she felt like it. She'd have to wait her turn. She gave the secretary her work phone number and added, on an impulse, "You can just tell him it's his partner in crime."

Would he guess who that was? Evidently not, because when Lily answered her phone an hour later, she heard a rather impatient voice saying, "This is Matt Malone. I have a message to call this number."

His brusqueness took her by surprise. She sat up a little straighter in her swivel chair, feeling irrationally glad that she'd worn her conservative navy-blue suit to work today. Maybe Matt couldn't see her, but it seemed somehow to put her on an equal footing with him.

"Is that any way to greet your fellow defendant?" she demanded. "I called to plot strategy with you. Have you got five minutes to spare?"

"Lily." The change in his tone was immediate. The instant that half humorous, half caressing sound came back to his voice, it was so easy to picture him—his thick, dark russet hair, and the way his mouth slid easily into a smile as though it were an embrace.

"What do you mean, plot strategy?" he was asking. "Do you know something I don't?"

His surprise sounded genuine. Briefly Lily outlined the letter she'd received in the mail two days before and waited through a brief silence that was loaded with question marks.

Finally he said, "I haven't heard anything about it yet, but I'm a couple of days behind in my mail. And I'm just about to go into another important meeting. Can I possibly call you back?"

Lily's joking mood was out the window by the time he finished speaking. Behind in his mail, more important meetings—all the red flags were showing, all right. If she wanted to have any dealings with Matt Malone, she'd have to take a number and wait in line. And she'd done far too much of that, far too recently.

"Sure," she said curtly. "I'll be here until five."

"Still doing the dull survey for the insurance company?" Matt asked.

"Yes." Lily was crowding all the coolness she could into her voice. He'd made it clear he had no time to talk now; let him save the small talk until there was nothing more important on his mind. "I'm sure you're very busy, Matt, so I won't keep you."

"Lily, wait," he said quickly. "Let me just look through my mail from yesterday. God, what a pile of paper! Here we go, this looks like it." She could hear him tearing open an envelope. There was another long pause.

"Hell," he said finally.

Lily said, "I agree."

"I hate this kind of lawsuit," Matt said. "It just clogs up the courts to no good purpose. What does she expect to get out of it, anyway?"

Lily suddenly felt perverse, thinking of Matt, and not Tommy Thompson, as the adversary. "I imagine she's just making a statement to show she's still a contender in spite of what a tough life she must lead. I have to admit I can admire that."

"I can't," Matt said flatly. "There are lots of other positive ways of making statements. This one just wastes everybody's time and money."

"Well, no matter what we may think about it," Lily said, "we're stuck with it. What do we do next?"

"Next we fire back a letter saying that it was Tommy Thompson's own fault she got hurt, and we have no intention of paying damages. And when they reject that, as I'm sure they will, they'll sue us."

"Do you think it will actually get to court?"

"Probably. To settle out of court, we'd have to agree to pay them something, and I'm assuming you don't intend to do that any more than I do."

"I sure don't. Do we want to hire a lawyer to take care of this?"

Matt laughed. "Seems unnecessary, doesn't it?" he asked. "I'll have to talk to my insurance company about it, of course, but I'm sure they'll let me handle it personally. My insurance agent is an old friend."

"My insurance won't enter into it," Lily said, "since I was walking, not driving. If we can't get Tommy to settle out of court, I guess I'd better get ready to fight."

"That's the spirit. We should get together on this, and be a jump ahead of old Tommy. Maybe we could meet in Boston some weekend and track down whatever witnesses the police have got."

It was like that moment when he'd kissed her, all over again. She knew she liked Matt a lot and wanted to know him better, and at the same time she was sure he would mean trouble if she let him into her life. If she hadn't been so badly burned by her last experience, she might be halfway to Boston by now. But she'd been this route before, and she knew the landmarks.

"I suppose you're used to working on weekends," she said.

"Sure." Lily could hear the smile in his voice. Was he laughing with her or at her? "I forgot you're the only lawyer in the world who sticks to a forty-hour work week," he added.

"I seem to remember you thought it was commendable," she said pointedly.

"Commendable, yes," he admitted. "Unfortunately, it's not always possible." She could hear the sound of pages flipping. "Let me see. I'm tied up for most of this month, but here's a meeting I could probably cancel, in a good cause. What do you say to the last weekend in October?"

Was it a hopeful sign that he was willing to cancel a meeting to see her? In spite of herself, she felt herself warming up to the idea. "I'll have to call you back," she hedged. "My calendar's at home."

She underestimated his persistence. "You know," he said, "I bet I know exactly what expression you're wearing at the moment. I'd bet anything you've got that No Trespassing look on your face, haven't you?"

Lily's frown deepened. Several men in the past had told her they found her attractive, but no one had ever said she had signs on her face. "What are you talking about?" she asked.

Matt chuckled. Apparently he'd managed to put his important meeting out of his mind. "I know you are," he said. "I can hear it in your voice, too. You're trying to tell me to stay out of your business. But now you've got me curious, and curiosity has always been a problem of mine. Why so adamant about keeping your free time free, Lily Martineau?"

Lily started to tell him it wasn't any of his business. Then she stopped. He was already ahead of her on that one. She leaned forward in her chair, her elbows on the desk. "My experience tells me," she said guardedly, "that once you start letting your work take over your life, it's tough to know where to stop."

She heard his inviting chuckle again, the one that said, "Let go a little bit and smile back at me." Lily made herself more serious to counteract its charm. If he could see her now, he'd be reading a whole field of No Trespassing signs.

"That's a nice, impersonal answer," he said. "Care to be a little more specific? What experience has made you so sure about this?"

He was getting entirely too near the bone. Damn Matt Malone for putting his finger so unerringly on her sorest spot! "It's nothing that would interest you," she told him. "Look, Matt, I should get back to work, and I know you're busy. Why don't you give me a call closer to the court date? I really don't think we need to be in touch before then."

Doors firmly shut and locked, she thought with satisfaction. But Matt seemed to know the back way in.

"Don't forget," he said smoothly, "our date for the last weekend of this month."

"We don't have a date for the last weekend of this month," she told him.

"Not even if I promise to take you out for a fancy dinner and spend an entire evening not talking about the law?"

"Not even then."

"Lily..." The disappointment in his voice was something she hadn't expected, and it tore away at her resolve. "I've been thinking about you day and night ever since last weekend. I can't tell you how many times I've picked up the phone to call you, but—"

She knew the answer to that one. "But you've been so busy with work," she finished for him. "It's all right, Matt. You don't have to make excuses."

"I'm not making excuses," he said. He sounded almost angry, maybe because she'd hit the mark. "Yes, I've been busy with work. But it's not as though I didn't have time to make a phone call. It's just that I didn't want to sandwich you in for whenever I have five free minutes. You mean more to me than that."

"That's what you're doing now," she pointed out.

"Ah, that's just because you snuck up on me," he said. "Caught me unawares. Come and visit me in Boston, and we'll spend some real time together. And we really should do some work on this case, you know.''

She knew. This lawsuit could cost her a lot of money she didn't have, and it was a personal matter, so it wasn't quite the same as bringing her job home with her on a weekend. She knew how much she wanted to see Matt again, too, and her conflicting instincts were tearing her apart. Attraction told her to say yes to his proposal; self-preservation told her to stay far away. She closed her eyes briefly and a mental picture came back to her: the strength of his body, the half teasing, half sensual smile on his face. Attraction gained a slight lead over self-preservation.

Lily's fingers tightened around the telephone receiver. If only his words didn't echo Alexander's so damnably! "If we get together, it's going to be strictly to work on our defense, then," she said firmly. "That has to be absolutely clear."

"You do like to have things all settled in advance, don't you?"

"I always have. If you don't state your terms at the beginnings of things, then misunderstandings happen."

"Good point." His unexpected agreement took the wind out of her sails. She was beginning to see what a formidable opponent he could be in a courtroom—or out of it. "All the more reason for us to get together. There's a misunderstanding between us that needs clearing up, and once it's cleared up, I think you might revise your opinion of me."

"What is it?" He'd piqued her curiosity, and she was drawn back to him in spite of herself.

"I can't tell you now. And I've really got to run. What do you say?"

"I suppose I could come up for a couple of hours on Saturday afternoon," she said, "and take you up on your offer of dinner."

He'd won a considerable victory, and he seemed wise enough to know it. "I'll take a couple of hours, with pleasure," he said. "Why don't we meet at two at my place?" He gave her the address.

Lily noted it down and added sternly, "If we meet at two, that gives us more than a couple of hours before dinner."

"It does, doesn't it?" Matt sounded surprised. "Well, in that case, we'll just have to fill up the time with a walk around the Common, or something."

"It'll probably rain." Lily was having a hard time keeping the laughter out of her voice. She'd never met anyone with such persistent charm.

"Then we'll stay inside in front of a crackling fire."

"You have a fireplace in your apartment?"

"Sure do. We can burn some old law books. That ought to keep you warm."

She was laughing with him by the time she hung up. And all the No Trespassing signs had already mysteriously vanished before she noticed it.

"Why not just wear jeans?" Sarah asked for the second time, and Lily sighed.

"I don't know," she hedged, staring into her closet as if looking for inspiration. "It just seems that since this is a business meeting, I should be businesslike."

It was the first Saturday morning in November, and Lily had called in her roommate to consult on what she should wear to her rendezvous with Matt. Lily had suggested one of her more casual suits, but Sarah had rejected that instantly as too formal.

"Is Matt Malone as gorgeous as I've heard he is?" she asked a trifle too casually.

Lily had to admit that he was. "Not that it matters," she added, "since I'm not interested in handsome lawyers anymore."

"Come on, Lily," Sarah prompted gently. She was one of the few friends who knew how painful Lily's broken engagement had been. "Not all handsome lawyers are carbon copies of Alexander Bartlett III."

"This one is," Lily said, pulling a black wool skirt and a ruby-red cowl-necked sweater out of the cupboard with sudden decisiveness. "Even worse. At least Alexander never carried a beeper around, and Matt does. Getting involved with him would be like romancing the entire firm of Sloan and Baker."

Sarah giggled. "It doesn't sound very appealing when you put it like that," she said. "But I still think you should stay for the whole weekend and have some fun. You owe it to yourself; you must be bored to death with that survey by now."

"Bored?" Lily looked at her friend in mock surprise. "On the contrary. It's the most exciting thing I've done since Professor Higginson's contract law class."

Professor Higginson, as Lily and Sarah had good cause to know, was a sleep inducer of legendary proportions.

"You know, we could corner the sleeping pill market if we could just bottle that class somehow," Sarah said. "Or your survey, for that matter."

"All right, I admit it's a little dull," Lily said. "But it's paying the bills for the moment, so I can't really complain. And it's coming along faster than I expected. I should be done by January, although I don't know if that's a good thing or not."

"Still no more job offers?"

"Just one, for part-time work that I can't afford to live on. No nice little local law firms wanting help these days, apparently."

"Well, there's a rumor that the insurance company is looking to hire a couple more people in my department. I'm sure you'd have a good shot at it since you're already there. I'll put in a word for you if a job comes up."

Lily had to smile as she finished brushing her thick dark hair. It was impossible to convince Sarah that all lawyers didn't want a career in an insurance firm or a bank.

"We'll see." Lily hedged. "*If* a job comes up."

Her smile faded a little as she spoke. If a job did come up, she might be wise to take it. She already had a place to live and a good friend as a roommate. And no one from her ideal law firm was knocking very hard at her door at the moment. But maybe she'd have tracked down that ideal firm by the time her temporary job here was finished. In the meantime she and Matt would just have to make sure they didn't get slapped with a settlement that she for one couldn't afford to pay. She had enough things on her mind without worrying about that, too.

"I don't imagine I'll be too late getting home tonight," she said. "Are you and Jimmy going anywhere fun and exciting?" Jimmy was a colleague from the insurance company, and Sarah's current companion.

Sarah made a wry face. "Probably just to the pizza place on the corner," she said. "We have some stuff to finish up at work, and it looks like it'll take all day."

Sarah, too, was starting to fit into Lily's stereotype of the workaholic lawyer. "Well, save me some pizza, then," she said. "I'm going out sketching tomorrow. It'll make me a picnic lunch."

"That reminds me," Sarah said. "Did you see the newspaper article I cut out for you? About the library's art exhibit?"

"I did." Lily took a quick look around her room at the several large watercolors that decorated the walls. "But I'm really not in that league, I'm afraid."

"What are you talking about? These are beautiful. And that big one on the living room wall is one of my favorite pictures. You ought to enter, Lily; I'm sure the jury would pick your paintings to put in the show."

"I've never really had the nerve to exhibit anything in public," Lily said honestly, "but thanks for the vote of confidence." She stepped into a pair of low-heeled black leather shoes and changed the subject abruptly. "How's this for a businesslike image?"

Sarah cocked her head critically. "As a compromise between jeans and a suit, just right," she pronounced. "Now, about that art exhibit—"

"You lawyers sure are a pushy bunch." Lily laughed, leading the way out of her bedroom and closing the door behind her. Lily's room was almost spartan in its neatness, so her watercolor landscapes were the natural focus of the room. Sarah, on the other hand, lived in a kind of tornado of piles of things that were always falling over, or threatening to. Their living room was a curious compromise, with areas of tidiness bravely fending off encroaching stacks of law books or laundry that Sarah hadn't sorted yet.

Lily looked around the room. She was comfortable here in spite of the difference between her style and Sarah's. Should she take a full-time job if it came up and stay in Hartford? Her recent experience with lawyers was making that perfect law firm seem more remote than ever.

Well, she'd decide that when the time came. She grabbed her car keys from the kitchen counter and headed down the stairs.

Lily's prediction of rain had come true. It was a dreary November day that Matt saw from the window of his second-floor Beacon Hill apartment. Most of the leaves had fallen, and the tall red-brick buildings seemed empty and gloomy. Across the street a neighbor had filled her window boxes with brilliant orange bittersweet berries, and the splash of color was a welcome sight.

His breath seemed to catch in his throat when he saw Lily's small white car pull into a parking space down the street. Stay calm, he reminded himself. He couldn't very well greet her on the doorstep by imprisoning her in his arms and demanding that she acknowledge the desire he'd felt in her when he'd held her close to him two weeks ago. It was better to start slowly. They were two lawyers working together, that was all. He'd let it be a professional relationship for now and see where things went.

"We used to be neighbors," she informed him when he opened the building's front door to let her in. "My old apartment was half a block from here."

"Think of the wasted opportunities," he said, leading the way up one flight of stairs and into his apartment.

"Opportunities for what?" There it was, that manner she had of putting him courteously at a distance. Matt could feel himself rising to the challenge of it already.

"To get to know each other," he said smoothly, taking her coat. Even the heavy black wool fabric smelled faintly sweet, the way he remembered her tasting. Damn, he thought. And I was going to be so cool and professional. How could he not kiss her, when just being near her was making him yearn to take her in his arms?

She didn't answer him right away, but surveyed the apartment with what seemed to be an approving look. The place spoke strongly of Matt. There was a solid dependability in the furnishings and art he had chosen, but also a certain flair that might have been a surprise to her, if she hadn't already suspected that there was much more to the man than met the eye. He was clearly partial to rich hues; the deep color of his carpet and solid oak of his furniture seemed to warm the room themselves. There was firewood—not law books—ready to light in the small fireplace.

"I doubt we would have gotten to know each other very well, Mr. Malone," Lily said. "I suspect we traveled in different circles."

Matt raised his eyebrows. So she was going to carry politeness to extremes, was she? It was exactly the kind of challenge he couldn't resist. "*Mr.* Malone?" he said. "I could have sworn we were on a first-name basis."

Lily turned to face him, looking him squarely in the eyes for the first time. "If we're going to have a business relationship, I think we should keep it businesslike," she said.

"I thought we were a little friendlier than that."

There was a look of determined courtesy in her face. "We can be as friendly as you like," she said, "within the limits of what we are."

"And what are we?"

"Co-defendants in a lawsuit."

"That's all?"

"Absolutely all."

"Funny thing." Matt let Lily's coat fall over the back of the sofa and moved closer to her. "I could have sworn there was something more than friendship in what you were feeling the last time we met."

Lily held her ground, wishing he wasn't quite so close. "I think you might have been mistaken," she said.

"I was quite sure of it at the time," he insisted, and then, in spite of all the lectures he'd given himself about taking lots of time to let things develop, he couldn't resist the longing he felt. She was too near and too desirable, and he needed to break through that reserve and reassure himself that the passion he'd sensed was still strong in her. He *couldn't* be wrong about it, not when he felt as he'd never felt with a woman before!

Lily had time for one quick intake of breath before he closed the distance between them. Then, when his body met hers, she became lost in a sweet rush of remembrance and desire. He felt so familiar—had she really been reliving their one embrace that often? The musky male scent of him filled her nostrils like a well-remembered perfume.

At first his mouth just teased, brushing hers in a mere shadow of a kiss. It roused a longing deep inside her, and she tilted her face up to his. He was gentle and forceful all at the same time, but at the first soft moan from the back of Lily's throat, he pressed closer, demanding more.

Her lips parted as though asking him inside, and she gave another involuntary moan when she met the warm, welcome invasion of his tongue. Vaguely she remembered that in some other incarnation she'd been trying to prevent this from happening, but at the moment she was lost in the delight of his lips and in answering his kiss with searching, hungry movements of her own. She shuddered from head to foot when he ran his tongue seductively along her lower lip, and groaned with still half-smothered desire.

His strong hands spanned her back, and her body felt slender and small in his grip. At the same time, she'd never been so aware of the strength inside herself, as though he'd called it up to match his own powerful body. She kissed him back again and again, astonished at her reactions, and finally cried out as he covered the smooth skin of her face and neck with light, maddening kisses.

Both of them were left gasping. Lily realized, the instant he lifted his head and looked at her, that she'd wanted the kiss to go on and on. She wanted to explore him with her hands and eyes—the strength of his shoulders, the rugged male beauty of his whole body. She was almost shocked at how much ground her wandering imagination had covered. Certainly she wasn't given to sensual fantasies about men she hardly knew! But something in Matt's curving lips not only inspired those fantasies but seemed to invite them also. What fantasies of his own lurked beneath that ghost of a smile?

This would never do. Lily took firm command of her breathing and reminded herself just exactly what the situation was here. Working together would be the excuse for lovemaking, at first. But all too soon, making love would turn into merely a fringe benefit of working together. Just because Matt aroused her in a way that was hard to resist, that was no reason to let her heart run ahead of her brain again.

He was still a lawyer. She reminded herself of the abrupt ending of their first embrace, when his beeper had gone off in her ear. Maybe there wouldn't be an interruption that graphic every time, but she knew that the interruptions would always be there. And that gave her a very good reason not to get entangled in another embrace once she'd extricated herself from this one.

"I didn't really plan that," he was saying, and the honesty in his voice nearly undid her resolve. "But you're so lovely, and I've been thinking about you so much."

He reached up and ran a hand through her hair. "Is it brown, or is it black?" he mused out loud. "This is the color I always imagined sable to be."

"I've always thought of it as just plain brown," Lily said, stepping back a pace away from his arms.

"There's nothing plain about you," he assured her. "Your eyes make me think of the color of dew first thing in the morning."

"I don't think dew has a color." She was trying to sound brusque, but his compliments were making her heart beat faster again, and she was sure he could see it in her face.

"All right, the color of the palest blue in an abalone shell, then." His smile told her he was refusing to be put off.

"I'd forgotten about your poetical streak, Mr. Malone."

"Oh, I have a lot of talents, Ms. Martineau."

And foremost were his legal abilities, she thought. With that, the spell was broken, to her immense relief. She was far too susceptible to this man, she knew.

"I smell coffee," she hinted.

"Coming up. Cream and sugar?"

"Just cream. Why is it that lawyers can never work unless they have coffee in front of them?"

"It's because we're born with caffeine in our veins, instead of good red blood."

As he spoke, Matt put two mugs of steaming coffee on the oak table, and they got down to work.

Five

There were two things that shook Lily up that afternoon.

The first was the discovery of just how well she and Matt worked together.

Although he was as brilliant and experienced as any lawyer she'd encountered, he made her feel more like his partner, not his pupil. They complemented each other in a way that was new to Lily. As Matt dug through his casebooks looking for precedents, Lily called the witnesses who had given statements to the police. When they'd pooled the information they'd come up with, Matt commented on what an effective team they were.

"We ought to do this more often," he said, sounding surprised and pleased. "We've gotten through three times as much as I could have done alone, or with anyone else."

Lily knew it was true, and she sighed, an angry little sound that made Matt look at her sharply. She couldn't face the thought of another partnership where work and romance overlapped, the way they had with Alexander. Love would inevitably be pushed into second place by a man who was completely caught up in his work.

That was made even clearer by the second thing that shook her up. The big oak table that Matt used as a desk was already covered with papers, books and file folders when Lily arrived. He seemed to have been hard at work for some time. Another weekend workaholic, Lily thought glumly.

He confirmed her suspicions as he pushed things aside to make room for her briefcase. "I thought I was going to have a free weekend," he said apologetically, "but something blew up at the last minute yesterday, and I've got to take care of it before a court appearance on Monday."

"Another important case?"

Matt paused for some reason. Then he said, "Well, according to Sloan and Baker, it is."

That was an odd answer, Lily thought. It was even odder that Matt seemed eager to change the subject as he turned his attention to the file folder in front of him. Something was definitely up. She remembered his promise that he was going to tell her something to change her opinion of him. If that was what he had up his sleeve, he was being unusually hesitant about it.

There was certainly nothing hesitant in the way he responded to Lily's suggestion that they might not need quite so many witnesses. He seemed to feel Tommy had insulted him and all his ancestors. "If she wants a fight, I'll make sure she gets one," he said.

"You seem to be taking this personally," she said.

"Do I?" He smiled at his own vehemence. "I suppose I feel as though she's challenged me on my own turf, somehow. *Our* turf, I should say. You're a lawyer, too, you should understand this."

"We're very different kinds of lawyers, Mr. Malone," she said.

"How so, Ms. Martineau?"

She wished he wouldn't mimic her every time she called him Mr. Malone. She knew he was poking gentle fun at her, trying to get her to loosen up, but it only made her more determined to resist his charm.

"We've been through this before," she told him. "I'm interested in the law as something that helps people. You're interested in building a career and a reputation. It's a big difference."

He started to answer and then seemed to change his mind. Lily glanced at the heaping piles of work on Matt's desk. Maybe he just realized that his obsession with his career spoke for itself.

They turned their attention back to Tommy, and the next time they paused, Lily was astonished to see that it was almost dark outside. Her watch read just past five o'clock.

"So much for our two hours of work," she said. "Did I mention my rates for overtime?"

"I'll be happy to pay up," he said. "Name your price."

It was obvious he wasn't talking about money, and she didn't want to get into what he *was* talking about. Clearly he had plans for their acquaintance to go places, and she was just as adamant that it would stay right where it was.

"I'll settle for dinner," she said lightly. "I've been fantasizing about smelling a roast in the oven for the past hour."

"That's because you *have* been smelling a roast in the oven for the past hour, thanks to the miracle of modern technology. I put a pork roast in earlier and set the timer to start cooking it at four. We can eat at six."

"We're having dinner here?" She hoped she didn't sound as startled as she felt. She'd been counting on moving to neutral ground, a restaurant somewhere, not spending the evening alone with Matt in his apartment.

"No need for alarm," he said, and she could have sworn he'd read her thoughts. "You're in the hands of a perfectly competent cook. My mother believed in boys learning to fend for themselves. I should warn you, though, that after tasting my stuffed pork roast, women have been known to fall on their knees and beg me to marry them."

Lily laughed. "I'm not the type to be falling on my knees, Mr. Malone."

"I can believe that, Ms. Martineau. Now come and sit in the kitchen while I make your dinner."

What type *are* you? Matt wanted to ask. More than ever, he wanted to take her in his arms and peel away the layers of defense she'd pulled around herself. He couldn't tell which need was more urgent, the peeling away of defenses or the taking of Lily in his arms.

He had to make do with basting the roast pork, and with an effort he managed to stop thinking of how attractive he found Lily's combination of independence and femininity, until he'd gotten dinner on the table.

The meal was half over before he got around to the subject he'd been working up to all afternoon. He tried to sound casual as he took away Lily's dinner plate and put a salad in front of her.

"Now that I've won your heart with my culinary magic, I have something to tell you," he said, sitting back down and looking into her eyes. "Which do you want to hear first, the good news or the bad?"

Lily looked up at him. She'd been admiring the appetizing-looking arrangement of vegetables on her plate, and she'd rather concentrate on her food than look into Matt's disturbingly direct brown eyes.

"Might as well start with the bad," she said.

"It's nothing terrible," he said hastily, seeing the look on her face. "I just wanted to warn you that there's a good possibility I'm going to have to take a business call before long. There's someone I've been trying to get hold of for several days, and the only time he's going to be near a phone is right about now, and—"

He seemed to be faltering, forcing the words out. Lily finished up for him. "I know, Matt," she said. "You wouldn't do it if it weren't important, and you have to talk to this person before your court appearance on Monday, and you promise it won't happen again." She spoke without bitterness, just a simple stating of the facts. "Have I missed anything?"

"Not a damn thing, I'm afraid. The only good thing is that you seem to have stopped calling me Mr. Malone."

"You don't have to apologize for being a busy man, Matt. I may not want to run my life that way, but it's not my business to tell you how to run yours."

"Maybe I don't want to run my life this way, either," he said unexpectedly. "Did you ever think of that?"

Lily frowned. She looked at the piles of file folders that Matt had pushed to one side so that there was room to eat at the table. "Then why—" she began.

Matt cut her off with an impatient hand. "That's the good news, Lily. Let me explain it all, from the beginning, and then maybe you'll be willing to give me a second chance."

Lily leaned back in her chair, watching him. He'd lit two tall candles when he'd served dinner, and in their soft light his face was more attractive than ever. Lily's fingertips tingled when she remembered the feel of his skin and the way his thick auburn hair curled a bit at the base of his neck. She could imagine running her fingers through those curls again....

She sat up straighter. She would imagine no such thing, not if she had any sense. Let him put his good news on the table first, and then she would reassess the situation.

"I went into law school with the same notions you did," he said, still looking directly into her eyes. "I wanted to be a legal white knight, helping people sort out their problems and maybe fixing a few injustices along the way."

"You make it sound like a pipe dream," she commented.

"Only because I'm such a grown-up now that I'm embarrassed to admit I still feel that way about the law," he said. "But I do, Lily, in spite of ten years of being a mouthpiece for big corporations and not really helping anybody the way I originally intended to."

"Now I'm really intrigued," she admitted. "How does a prospective white knight turn into a corporate mouth-piece?"

"Sheer dumb luck. When I got out of school, I was in the same situation you're in now. I wanted a satisfying job, but I had loans to pay off and a landlord who couldn't wait forever for the first month's rent. So I applied to a lot of fancy firms, figuring I'd get myself solvent first, and then pursue my high-minded career. I was in the office at Sloan and Baker, dropping off my résumé, when Derek Sloan came in, arguing with one of the other partners about a case. I don't know if you know anything about Derek."

"I know he has a reputation for not being a very good loser," Lily said.

"That's it in a nutshell. You cross Derek at your own peril. But in this argument, he was wrong, and I knew he was wrong. The other partner was probably smart enough to know what would happen if he argued too hard, and was deferring to Derek. But I wasn't that smart, and I chimed in with the precedent that proved Derek wrong."

Lily smiled. "Talk about fools rushing in where angels fear to tread."

"Well, no one ever accused me of being shy and retiring. Anyway, for a few seconds I thought Derek was going to throw me out of the place, and then he started to laugh. It turns out he has a quirky sense of humor in spite of being such a cantankerous character. And he liked the idea that here was this kid barely out of law school, who was brash enough to challenge Derek Sloan himself while applying for a job with Derek Sloan's firm. It doesn't happen often."

"I can believe it."

"Well, the result was that he hired me on the spot and took me under his wing. He'd decided that I had what it took to be a first-rate courtroom lawyer, and he saw to it that I got all the help and experience I needed along the way. I may be good at what I do, but I wouldn't be nearly as good without the advice and opportunities I got from Derek."

"That wouldn't be an easy opportunity to turn down," Lily mused.

Matt seemed relieved that she understood. "That's exactly it," he said. "I still had this notion that I was going to start from scratch some day, with a little storefront law firm, but in the meantime, more and more important cases were getting thrown my way, and it was hard to refuse them. I liked the experience, I was bitten by the challenge, and the money was nice, too. And I was grateful to Derek, who'd spent a lot of his time helping me. I couldn't just walk out on him."

"It's funny," Lily said. "Most people work and scheme and flog themselves half to death to get where you are now. And you just sort of stumbled into it."

"Sheer dumb luck, as I said."

"I can see that. But—"

"I haven't come to the good part yet." He leaned forward, elbows resting on the table. His dark brown eyes glittered in the candlelight, alive and intelligent. "I've never really given up on that old dream of my one-man storefront operation in some little town somewhere. And this past summer I finally made the decision to leave Sloan and Baker and set up on my own. I've bought property in Brattleboro, Vermont, and by spring next year I'm hoping to be completely moved there and working for myself."

"But what about all of this?" Lily indicated the piles of paper on Matt's table.

"I made a deal with Derek. I told him what I wanted to do, and after he'd called me an idealistic fool and a lot of other things, he said I could go with his blessing, but he'd appreciate it if I'd finish up some important things before I went. He also asked me not to spread the word yet that I was leaving. My name is sort of a draw at Sloan and Baker, and he wanted to recruit some people to cover the kind of work I've been doing."

Lily looked around Matt's apartment again. There were still the stacks of work he'd brought home, and the law

books open where he'd left them. Was it really possible for
such a stereotypical corporate lawyer to change his stripes
the way Matt was proposing to do?

"Tell me more about your new law practice," she said.

"Cautious, aren't you? I thought once you heard I was
leaving Sloan and Baker you'd revise your opinion of me on
the spot."

"I've learned to be cautious, Matt. If I'd been a little
more cautious this past year, I wouldn't have been—" She
stopped herself. She didn't want to get into that with Matt.
Not now and maybe not ever. "What kind of work are you
planning to do in Brattleboro?"

"The kind you and I both went into law to do." His
shrewd eyes must have seen her near-confession, but he
seemed to have decided to let it go for the moment. "Little
things, like wills and real estate transactions. And some
bigger things. For instance, I've been approached by one of
the small colleges up there about a pending lawsuit that
could cost them a lot of money. But no more big corporations. I want to deal with people for a change, not just with
other attorneys."

"Attorneys and people being two different things?" Lily's
dimples showed briefly when she smiled at the notion.

He smiled back. "There are days when I think that might
be true," he admitted. "Well, what do you think?"

She considered for a moment. "To be perfectly honest
about it, I'm having a hard time picturing you settling down
to a career defending Mr. Jones against Mr. Smith because
Mr. Jones let his dog dig up Mr. Smith's peonies," she said.

"That's what Derek said, too."

He was leaning toward her, and once again Lily had to
fight against the power that drew her to him. She wanted to
lean her own elbows on the table, as he was doing, and feel
those strong, warm hands close over hers.

"What if Derek Sloan and I are both right?" she asked.

Matt shrugged. His handsome face was philosophical and
humorous. "Then I can always get a job with another fancy

firm," he said. "But both you and Derek seem to be underestimating me. I've wanted to do this for a long time, and I fully intend to succeed."

Something in the set of his jawline made Lily believe him. It also made her wonder even more if a man of Matt's strength and determination really would be satisfied drawing up wills in a quiet town. He had ambition stamped all over him.

"So this law firm will be just you—no partners, no clerks, no nothing?" she asked him.

"That's the idea. If I get busier than I want to be, I'll just stop taking on more work. It's one of the reasons I want to leave Sloan and Baker. I'm tired of having someone else decide my schedule for me. But I still haven't told you the best part—"

The shrill ringing of the telephone cut Matt off. He slammed his open hand on the oak table. "Cue the phone," he said, sounding angry. "Lily, I'll be as quick as I can."

"At least I was warned," Lily said as Matt pushed back his chair and walked to the phone. Lily stayed seated, looking down at the salad in front of her as though she could sort things out by studying the patterns in the lettuce leaves and pepper rings.

She was surprised at her own confusion. She'd fully intended to be detached and distant, keeping Matt Malone at arm's length. But now, with his surprising confession about leaving his high-powered job, he'd managed to wear down her resolve, so that in the back of her mind she was already reconsidering her first impressions of him and wondering if it might be possible to follow her instinctive attraction to him after all.

And then, just as that treacherous thought had come along, duty had called Matt away again. Would it always happen that way, she wondered, no matter who he was working for? She was afraid that it would, and there was no way she wanted to take a chance on being hurt by that all over again.

She kept staring at her plate. They'd been on the verge of turning this evening into a relaxed, friendly interlude. And now it was just another meal squeezed in between bouts of legal business. She'd eaten so many meals like that, and she remembered the taste of all of them—bitter.

"Actually, I had made plans for tomorrow," she heard Matt saying. "No, nothing I can't change, I suppose. No, you're right. We do have to wrap this up before Monday, and if I have to get those files from you anyway, I might as well meet with Donald at the same time."

He sounded frustrated, Lily thought. Then she stiffened her resolve. It wasn't her problem, she told herself. She refused to let Matt Malone's professional life enter her own.

"All right, ten o'clock at your place. Make sure there's plenty of coffee." Matt seemed to be having a harder time than usual being charming. Even his smile looked strained as he hung up the phone.

"One more call," he said apologetically, "and I promise I'll take the thing off the hook while we finish our dinner."

The one more call dragged on. Matt spoke with someone and then waited. "His wife has to go find him," he explained to Lily, one hand over the receiver.

Lucky woman, Lily thought. Spending her Saturday evening running business messages for her husband.

"Donald," Matt said at last. "Sorry to bother you. But Jack has come up with those files we needed, and he thinks we should get together tomorrow, before the court appearance on Monday."

He did sound truly sorry to Lily's ears. But that hadn't prevented him from making the call. When he finally sat down at the table again, having unplugged the telephone first, Lily's mind was made up. *No more lawyers* had been a good rule in the first place, and she intended to stick with it.

"I probably just lost all the points I gained earlier, didn't I?" he said. He could be unnervingly accurate sometimes, Lily was discovering.

"It doesn't matter," she said lightly. "I understand you have commitments, and—"

Matt had already picked up his fork again. Now he put it down and reached over to take her small chin in his hand. His grip was firm, bordering on threatening. "When you get that polite look on your face, I want to grab you and shake you," he said.

His touch wasn't threatening—it was demanding and challenging and arousing. The sound in his voice wasn't anger, it was desire, and the instant his fingers met her skin, they both knew it.

He slid his hand down her long neck, and she heard her own sudden intake of breath. His touch was so warm and so sure. His hand stopped at the base of her neck, resting on her bulky cowl-necked sweater, but her imagination kept going until all of her skin trembled in anticipation.

"That's better," he said roughly, and Lily knew that she was looking anything but polite. "Now listen up, because I'm going to tell you the rest of my story, and when I'm done I have a question that needs answering."

"You—you said you hadn't gotten to the best part yet." Lily's heartbeat was thumping in her ears. She wanted desperately to turn her face slightly and caress the warm center of his palm where it was resting against her neck. She'd never met a man who could make her forget every good intention so suddenly.

"That's right." He leaned back, withdrawing his hand slowly and seeming to enjoy the confusion on Lily's face. "The best part of moving is that since June I've been building myself a house up in Vermont. A big log cabin, full of skylights and fireplaces and with a view to kill for."

"Mountains?" Lily forced herself to concentrate on the picture he was painting.

"Mountains and forest and a stream," he said. "I finally got all the outer walls done last month, and the windows were installed a week ago. So it's snug enough and just waiting for the indoor finishing work to be done."

"It sounds wonderful," she said.

"It *is* wonderful," he said, and Lily had to smile with him at his own enthusiasm. "I've always lived in apartments and other people's houses. But this is a place I really want to go back to at the end of the day, a place worth spending your free time in."

"And there must be such satisfaction in building it yourself."

"That's exactly it. By the time the place is finished, I'll have had my hand in virtually every corner of it. No court case I ever tackled has given me the same kind of proud feeling."

"When you talk about spending your free time there," Lily said slowly, "does that mean you're planning to have more free time to spend?"

The look of satisfaction on Matt's face was still growing. "Absolutely," he said. "Which brings me to the question I said you were going to have to answer."

"What's that?"

"Will you come to Brattleboro with me some day soon and see the place and the office I'm setting up? So far you've only seen me when I'm up to my neck in Sloan and Baker's business. I'm a different person in real life, believe me."

Lily wanted to believe him, but her reservations were far too strong.

"The first time I met you, you were rushing off to Vermont on business of your own," she reminded him. "That didn't have anything to do with Sloan and Baker, did it?"

"No," he said, "but if I hadn't been still busy with Sloan and Baker's cases here, I wouldn't have been so frazzled about getting out of Boston."

"All right, but my point is that you were still dashing off into the wild blue yonder because a client had called you. That doesn't sound so different from letting a law firm dictate what your schedule is going to be."

"Damn it, Lily, this was important. My client needed advice in a hurry, and—"

Uncharacteristically he let his argument peter out. Maybe he'd sensed that he'd said just what she had expected him to say. There was an uncomfortable pause and then Matt remarked, "I guess I'm not doing such a great job of changing your mind about me, am I?" He sounded subdued, she thought.

"I'd love to change my mind," she said sincerely. "And you're so persuasive that you can almost do it when you talk. But when you stop talking and I look at the facts, I think I'm still right. You're just as tied up in your job as any lawyer I know, and I can understand why that is, but I'm certainly not going to share it."

"Things are going to change when I move," he insisted.

"I'm not holding my breath."

"Do you always decide on the verdict before the trial starts?" he demanded.

"But the trial *has* started, Matt. It started the day we met, and everything that's happened since then has confirmed what I thought in the first place—you're far too involved with your job for me to want to be involved with you."

"I think you're basing that on some unhappy experience in the past," he challenged her, "and I seem to be guilty by association."

"That's no business of yours," she flashed back. "And I'm basing it on one thing only—evidence. All the evidence shows that I'm right. I can see facts when they're under my nose, Matt, it's one of the things lawyers are trained to do."

"You want evidence? I think there's a big piece of evidence you're overlooking." Matt got to his feet and circled the end of the long table before Lily had a chance to react. He sounded almost angry, and his touch, when he pulled her up from her chair, was anything but gentle.

"Don't forget to take this into account," he muttered just before his lips closed over hers. There was a fierce possessiveness in the way his tongue invaded the softness of her mouth. For a second Lily fought back against his strength, resenting the way he was bullying her. But her resistance was lost in the scent of him and the sweet rush of desire that welled up in her at the intimate way his mouth was exploring hers.

Not only his mouth, but all of him seemed determined to prove to her just how good they felt together. She was aware of the whole length of his long, strong body, from the tensed shoulder muscles under her fingertips to the knotted hardness of his thighs against her legs. Her skirt and Matt's trousers might have been made of gossamer for all the protective barrier they provided. She was tormented by the need to feel even more of him, and to know what his skin would feel like alongside the softness of hers.

She knew Matt was having exactly the same thoughts. His hands slid from her waistline down over the roundness of her hips and settled with devastating sureness on the soft curve of her bottom. "Matt..." she said breathlessly, starting to frame a protest and hearing her voice come out as an entreaty. She wanted to give in completely to the desire that was coursing through her veins.

He moved his hands even lower, following the shape of her inner thighs. He seemed to sense the way the deep core of her body was pulsing in response to his touch, and to know exactly where that touch would be most irresistible. He shifted his position slightly, and Lily could feel the strength of his arousal, as instant and unbearable as her own.

She had forgotten why he'd kissed her in the first place, but apparently Matt hadn't. After what seemed like a very long time, he raised his head and looked at her. Through her own half-opened eyes, she could see that his eyes were dark with passion, and she knew from his breathing that his heartbeat was as wild and erratic as hers.

"You may think the evidence all points one way," he said hoarsely, "but if you ask me, I think there's a pretty strong case to be made for the two of us getting involved, too. And I think I just proved it beyond a reasonable doubt.''

Slowly Lily disentangled herself from his arms and took a step backward, away from the seduction of his embrace. Her hand encountered the oak chair she'd been sitting in when Matt had pulled her to her feet, and she dropped into it gratefully. Her knees felt a little less than trustworthy just at the moment.

''I can see where you got your reputation,'' she said, trying for flippancy and not quite succeeding. ''You can be very persuasive, when you put your mind to it.''

There was a satisfied smile on Matt's face as he sauntered back to his own side of the table. ''Does that mean I've changed your mind?'' he asked.

''No, it doesn't,'' she said promptly. ''It would be pointless to deny, well, that there's something between us. But that doesn't change the basic situation.''

His satisfaction dimmed a little, and Lily thought again that Matt wasn't a man who was comfortable with failure. Maybe his brilliance as an attorney stemmed from the fact that he just hated to lose.

''Well,'' he said philosophically, ''if the stuffed pork roast didn't do it, and the kiss didn't do it, I guess I'll just have to rely on Grandma Malone's Chocolate Mud Cake. No one's *ever* been able to resist that. Now eat your salad, or you don't get any dessert.''

For the rest of the meal, they managed to talk about small things, like recipes and apartment rentals and the difficulties of parking your car on Beacon Hill. The subject of law never came up, and Lily was amazed at how comfortable it felt to be chatting with Matt across his dining room table. There were so many sides to him, she thought—aggressive lawyer, demanding lover and now easygoing companion.

The problem was, she couldn't believe that the last facet of his personality was a permanent one. He'd unplugged the phone, true, but not until after he'd taken his important business call. And that call had caused him to change

whatever plans he'd had for tomorrow. Lily had had enough
of weekend vacations that had gotten canceled at the last
moment, dinners that had been delayed until she hadn't
been hungry anymore—and a wedding date that had been
put off several times for a more convenient time until it had
been canceled altogether, leaving a hurt inside her that was
far from healed.

No, she would never take up with another work-driven
lawyer, and Matt showed all the signs of being that kind of
lawyer. So she thought she was ready for his next onslaught
once they'd finished their dessert. She couldn't deny their
attraction, but she could keep it from going any further.

She was sure he'd try again to talk her into a visit to Vermont. He was too persistent a man to let the subject drop.
And she was right, but the tactic he used surprised her.

"You know," he said, "I went to boarding school in
Vermont, so I got to see it in every season of the year. And
nobody believes me when I tell them this, but I think I enjoy November there more than any other month."

"Why November?"

"There's something about the air then that I like. It's after the leaves are gone and before the snow's started, and
everything seems very clear and open. You can see things
you can't see any other time. And the light seems very pure,
somehow."

If there was one thing that intrigued a painter, it was talk
about light. Lily half wished she hadn't told Matt about her
hobby of painting. She suspected he was using it to bait his
hook and get her interested in his house in Vermont in spite
of herself.

The really annoying thing was that if that was what he was
doing, it was working. Lily wanted to know more. "I always thought of November as kind of dingy and dull," she
said. "Or just like all the other months, the way it is in California."

"Not in Vermont, it isn't," Matt told her. "Why don't
you come and see for yourself? If not to see me, then to

sketch or paint, or just wander around and look at the scenery. I think you'd like the mountains; they look as though they've been there since the beginning of time."

Lily was beginning to suspect Matt of being a wizard in finding people's weak spots. No wonder Sloan and Baker hated to let him go, she thought. She'd always had a buried hankering for old, green mountains, and now here he was dangling them in front of her. And she hadn't been on a real sketching expedition for a long while.

"And if you liked Grandma's Chocolate Mud Cake, there's a little restaurant outside of Brattleboro that you'd love," Matt went on, pressing his advantage. "They specialize in serious doses of chocolate. And somehow you look to me like a woman who can eat desserts and get away with it."

It was true—Lily had never had to worry about her waistline. But how did Matt know that?

There was no reason for her not to drive up to Vermont on her own any time she pleased, she knew. But it was the thought of Matt's company that made the whole idea so appealing. And at the same time, that was what made her hesitate.

"You're right, it does sound like something I would enjoy," she said, not wanting to commit herself yet. "I'll think about it and maybe later in the month—"

Matt cut her off. "If we let it go, we'll never get around to it," he said authoritatively. "At least, that's how things always work for me. We should set a date now, and I'll guard it with my life. Actually, I was hoping to talk you into going tomorrow, since the weather's supposed to clear up, but now this Sloan and Baker business is going to take up the whole day."

"And what if we set a date and another urgent case comes up?" Lily asked him.

"It won't," he said. His smile was positive, almost cocky. He was definitely a man who liked to have his own way, and now that he'd gotten it, he was clearly pleased. "I'll make sure of that. How about two weeks from today?"

Lily consulted her date book. "My roommate and I have a tentative date to hit some of the galleries in New York on that weekend," she said. "Sarah's convinced I know everything about art, and she's been picking my brains. But we can do that on Sunday, I suppose, and I could go to Vermont on Saturday."

Matt's smile broadened. "I'll call you sometime the week before, with directions," he said. "I'm assuming you'll be chained to your desk between nine and five every day?"

"That's an apt description of it. You know, it's a relief to admit to someone just how boring my job really is."

"All the more reason why you should have a day in the country," Matt said.

He was right yet again. A long walk in the mountains would take away the stale feeling that her temporary job always left her with by Friday afternoon.

And, a little voice kept whispering at her, *you can see what Matt's like when he gets away from his own work*. He was too cagey to press that point again, but Lily knew it was in both their minds. This was more than just a sketching expedition. It was a little victory for Matt in his campaign to change Lily's mind about him.

Because she knew he'd scored a victory, Lily was more careful than ever to be cool and polite when she thanked him for dinner and said goodbye. If she gave way too far, Matt's seductive charm would take over and she'd be lost.

"My compliments to the chef," she said, standing in the doorway, "and I'll see you in two weeks."

"Don't I get a goodnight kiss?" Matt asked. "I could pass it along to the chef, with your compliments."

Lily hesitated and then quickly stood on tiptoe and kissed Matt's cheek. It was anything but erotic, but even the brief scent of his skin and the sense of his nearness made her heart race.

"We don't want to get the chef too excited," she said, smiling at his disappointed face. "He has to keep his mind on his work, after all."

And then she was out the door, wondering if Matt felt the same ache that she did whenever they touched. If only she could give in to that longing . . .

But she knew she would be crazy to do that. She made herself forget the sensations that had run through her when Matt had held her in his arms, and by way of compensation, set her sights firmly on the clear November air of Vermont and their date for two weeks from today.

Six

Knowing Matt, Lily had half expected him to charm the weather into doing what he wanted. When the Saturday they'd set for their meeting in Vermont turned out to be gray and cloudy, she found herself feeling vaguely surprised.

Matt had sent her a key to his log house the week before. He'd called, too, with directions. He'd also called twice more to make sure she hadn't changed her mind, and once apparently just to see how she was. Then yesterday he'd called once more, to remind her to take the key and the directions, to make sure she hadn't changed her mind and to see how she was.

"As if I couldn't remember a simple set of directions," she fumed as she hung up the phone after the last call.

"I don't think it's the directions he's worried about," Sarah commented.

Lily sighed, knowing her friend was right. She wished Matt wasn't quite so persistent. She already knew he was charming, persuasive and appealing. It was the rest of him she was worried about. And if she let herself be bowled over by his charm, persuasiveness and appeal, what would happen if he turned out to be more interested in his career than in romance after all?

She knew exactly what would happen, having had it happen to her once already. "If he calls again," she said to Sarah, "tell him I'm in an important meeting and won't be done till ten tonight. That ought to stop him in his tracks."

He hadn't called again. And he hadn't arranged the weather, either, Lily thought as she drove north on the highway between Hartford and Brattleboro. The clear November light he'd sold her on was replaced by dull, overcast gray, and the low clouds looked unfriendly. Still Lily had to admit he'd been right about the beauty of the area. It felt good to be surrounded by trees and the rolling, rounded mountains.

They'd arranged to meet at ten, and Lily pulled up the long, wooded drive toward Matt's house almost exactly on time. There was no sign of his black Jeep yet, and she was glad she'd gotten there first. She had a feeling she would know more about him by studying the place where he'd chosen to settle, and it would be easier to do that by herself.

His property was well outside Brattleboro, and the house was set back from a little-used road. It was clearly brand-new, but its log walls gave it an old-fashioned look. At first glance it seemed small, but then Lily noticed the long, rambling wing at the back, and the second-story dormers and skylights, and realized that the place must be enormous inside.

Why had Matt built such a big place? she wondered. Well, he was a rich man after all. He could afford whatever kind of home he wanted. She was suddenly curious to see the inside.

She stepped up on the broad porch and opened the front door with the key Matt had sent. Inside, the place was almost eerily empty. There was rough plywood on the floors and windows set into the log walls, but everything else was unfinished. Still she could see the potential of the place, with its high cathedral ceilings and numerous windows. Even the cold, thin November light seemed to fill the place and warm it a little.

It wasn't quite efficient enough in the heating department, Lily thought, pushing her hands into the pockets of her jeans. She was wearing a bulky denim-blue sweater that had been enough in Hartford, but the late autumn chill seemed to go right through it now. She looked at the big stone fireplace that was the center of the main room and remembered Matt telling her at least three times that she should make herself at home. Did that include lighting a fire if she felt cold? She debated and looked at her watch. Quarter past ten. Matt would be here before long; she decided to wait for him. A fire always seemed cozier when there was someone to share it with.

She settled for fetching her navy-blue jacket from the car and putting it on. She was just climbing the front steps again, somewhat warmer and laden with sketchbooks and paint boxes, when she heard the phone ringing.

She'd noticed the phone as soon as she'd stepped into the house. It sat on the edge of the wide stone hearth, and she'd been mildly surprised to see it. Then she'd reminded herself that the telephone line was a lawyer's umbilical cord; of course a busy attorney like Matt would have a phone wherever he was.

Now it was ringing, and she had to decide whether to answer it or ignore it. If it was a business call for Matt at ten o'clock on a Saturday morning, she didn't really want to know about it. On the other hand, it might be Matt himself, calling for her.

She wasn't sure she wanted to know about that, either. Whenever she heard a phone ringing, she automatically assumed it was someone calling to cancel something she'd looked forward to. She'd had two years of it with Alexander, and it had made her a bit prone to jump to conclusions.

Maybe it was time to start changing that. She put down her books and boxes and picked up the telephone.

"Lily." There was so little of the usual self-confident charm in Matt's voice that at first she wasn't quite sure it was really he. Her heart was already sinking as she heard him say her name. His voice was full of apology, and she knew what that meant.

"Lily, I tried to reach you in Hartford, but you'd already left. I'm sorry as hell about this, but—"

"Where are you, Matt?"

"Still in Boston, but I'm just about to leave now. I should be there by noon, before, if I break a few speed limits."

"Don't tell me, an important client called."

"More or less. What happened was that Derek called me—"

"Spare me the details." Lily didn't want to hear any more. She was sure Matt's explanation was perfectly reasonable. She understood the delays and the cancellations. It was just that she didn't want to live with them.

"Lily, you have to believe that I wouldn't dream of doing this to you if I were working for myself," Matt was saying, and some of the warmth was coming back into his voice now. "If it had been anyone but Derek, I would have told them to forget it because I had a date with a lovely lady who thinks free time should be kept free. Will you try to pretend this hasn't happened, and that we arranged to meet at noon instead of at ten?" he asked.

"I don't know if I can. It's not just the two-hour delay, Matt. It's—there's a lot more to it than that."

"I can tell that there is. When I finally get there, will you explain it to me?"

She paused. All her instincts told her to cover up, but maybe Matt should know the whole story. If it wasn't going to work between them, he deserved to know why at least.

"I might," she hedged, hearing a suspicious quaver in her
voice. She knew that if she was smart, she'd get into her car
and get out of here right now. Carrying on with Matt would
only make things hurt much more. But now that they were
actually talking, she had to admit how close she felt to him
and how she'd looked forward to this visit. She felt a twist
of pain inside and wished fiercely that her feelings weren't
pulling her two ways like this.

His voice was gentle now, as if he knew what she felt.
"Will you still be there when I finally show up?" he asked.

"I might be," she said again. She was aware that she was
holding the telephone tightly enough to throttle it. "Goodbye, Matt." She hung up politely and firmly. She hadn't
decided yet just what her next step would be. But one thing
was clear—she didn't want to sit around in Matt's empty
new house for two hours, wallowing in old, unhappy memories. And she'd come to paint, anyway. She could do that
just as well without Matt. With a glance at the gravel-gray
clouds above, she buttoned her corduroy jacket for extra
warmth, picked up her drawing materials and headed for the
hills.

Matt was basically a law-abiding person, but he was sure
a stranger would never have known that from the way he
covered the distance from Boston to Brattleboro. He broke
speed limits from the instant he put his foot down on the
Jeep's accelerator and drove as though no one had ever told
him there were such things as state policemen.

Ever since his last meeting with Lily, he'd been thinking
hard about the things she had told him. She'd been very
specific about what she wanted out of life, and very vague
about a lot of other things. He felt as though he was operating in the dark. He needed more information from Lily if
he was going to get anywhere with this relationship he
wanted so much.

He'd also been thinking about the things she'd said about
him. That he was too caught up in his career to be able to

draw a line between work and play. That a change in his surroundings wasn't going to mean a change in his attitude.

He'd been surprised how much her criticisms had rankled, and it had taken him the better part of a week to admit to himself that they bothered him because they might be true. Somehow his life had become a part of his career, instead of the other way around. He hadn't intended for that to happen, and it had taken Lily's honest appraisal to wake him up to himself.

Now he had to convince *her* of that. He glanced at the back seat of the Jeep, at the picnic cooler that he'd filled with their lunch. Leaning against it was the sign he'd managed to have carved in a hurry this week. Maybe that would change her mind about him for good.

He was almost halfway across Massachusetts before it started to snow. At first the flakes were tiny, and he thought he was imagining them. Too late a night looking at documents, he thought, and not enough coffee this morning. No wonder he was seeing spots.

But before long the white spots turned more definitely into snow, and Matt fluently cursed to himself when he saw the white beginning to build on the side of the road. So much for the pure November light, he thought. He was really falling through on all his promises. Chances were, Lily would have decided he wasn't worth it. She would be gone by the time he got there, and he would have made the long trek for nothing.

He knew he didn't mean that. He knew perfectly well he'd drive farther for a chance at seeing Lily than for the certainty of seeing any other woman. And if she'd left, well, maybe he'd just follow her to Hartford. He'd never minded the snow, and the Jeep had four-wheel drive. He gritted his teeth, turned on the windshield wipers and nudged the accelerator a little closer to the floor.

At first Lily didn't believe it was snowing. Even though she was looking intently at the landscape as she sketched, it took her a while to realize that the slight fuzziness in the air was actually snow. She reached down to brush a wet spot off her sketchbook and felt another flake land on the back of her hand.

It's too early for snow, she thought, sitting up straighter on her folding camp stool. She stretched her shoulder muscles, looked at her watch and was surprised to see that she'd been sketching for almost two hours. She'd hiked for half an hour along what seemed to be an old trail through the woods, and it had led her to a viewpoint of such stunning beauty that she'd been busy drawing it from different angles ever since. She'd finally captured it to her satisfaction, she thought, flipping back through her sketchbook. She would get some good paintings from this.

Usually Lily concentrated completely on her drawing, blocking out anything else that might have been on her mind. It was one of the things she loved about this hobby and one of the reasons it gave her such a feeling of peace. But today Matt Malone had kept intruding on her thoughts no matter how hard she'd tried to ignore him. The strength of his arms, the sudden glint of his smile—everything about him stayed persistently with her. It made her angry, and more than once she'd caught herself muttering out loud as she sketched the mountains with uncharacteristically short, brisk strokes of her pencil. Matt had no right to march into her life and disrupt it like this.

Once the snow started in earnest, Lily packed up her equipment and folded the camp stool into its little carrying bag. She'd had it since her childhood days when she and her parents used to take hikes together. Her portable easel, too, had been a gift from her mother and father. When she was out drawing like this, she almost felt as though she was part of a family again. Would she ever be able to recapture the sense of belonging and completeness she'd known before her parents' sudden deaths?

Not with Matt Malone, she wouldn't. A man who couldn't even put his work aside for a simple Saturday in the country was hardly likely to be able to spare the time that a truly two-sided relationship took, not to mention the demands in time and patience required to raise a family. It was too bad, but Lily knew she had to face the facts. As she'd told Matt, that was one of the things lawyers were good at.

She was so busy thinking of Matt that she left the rocky place where she'd been sketching without really noticing if the trail she was taking was the same one she'd arrived on. A few minutes later she began to wonder if she was heading in the right direction.

Of course things wouldn't look the same, she told herself reasonably. She'd been looking at them from the other side two hours ago. Still she remembered a couple of large boulders and a stand of birch trees that she'd expected to see again by now.

She stopped and looked up at the sky. The gray clouds were lower than ever, and the snow had changed from occasional flakes to a fine lacelike haze in the air. The breeze that had been gentle earlier in the day was picking up now, stirring the dead leaves at Lily's feet. Did it snow much up here in November? Surely Matt would have warned her if it did.

She smiled at that thought. She couldn't pin *everything* on Matt just because she was mad at finding herself running a distant second to a legal case yet again. She decided to turn back, find the lookout spot again and see if the start of the trail looked familiar to her from there.

That was easier said than done. Somehow the simple act of turning around confused her sense of direction, and to make matters worse, the breeze had rearranged the leaves so she couldn't simply follow her footprints as she'd been hoping to do.

The snow was definitely thicker now, and the bare patches of ground were starting to turn to white. Lily made herself stop and take a deep breath, knowing that the worst thing

would be to go charging off without thinking. She squinted
up at the gray sky but couldn't pinpoint the position of the
sun, not that it would have done her much good if she had.
She'd never been a very good Girl Guide. Keep calm, she
told herself, but a little nudge of fear deep inside canceled
out her own advice.

She stood and listened for what seemed like a long time,
hoping for the sound of a car or truck. But all she heard was
the rising wind and the small pit-pit-pit of snowflakes hitting dead leaves. It was a pretty scene, but even with her
painter's eye, Lily wasn't in a mood to appreciate it. She had
no real sense of how far away Matt's house was, or if there
were other homes in the area. She had a vague notion of
walking until she found a road or a building, and then she
remembered the quiet emptiness of the hillsides she'd seen
on the drive in. Matt might live fairly close to a major center, but there was still a lot of countryside between here and
Brattleboro.

It would really cap off the day if she was lost! With the
firm intention of not letting that happen, Lily decided to go
back rather than forward and started toward what she
fondly hoped was the lookout place.

Half an hour later, she'd decided that the lookout place
must have moved and left no forwarding address. At least
she couldn't find it, and in the process of looking she'd
gotten herself completely turned around. She had no idea
which direction to try next. In short, she was lost.

She refused to say the word to herself yet. But she was
starting to feel a bit nervous with the tall trees all around her
and the rustling leaves underfoot, and no way to know
which way was forward. And the ever-thickening snow was
blurring things so that no matter which way she turned,
everything looked the same.

Her watch told her it hadn't been an hour since she'd left
the lookout spot, but it felt as though she'd been wandering without direction for a good half day. There was a
constant tremor of anxiety in her stomach now, and she

couldn't keep herself from looking ahead and envisioning the outcome of getting lost in a strange place in the snow in November, when the nights came early and got very cold. Could a person spend a whole night outside and not freeze to death? Lily looked around for some kind of shelter and saw only boulders and tree trunks—scanty shelter from the wind that was nipping at her face and gloveless hands.

"Damn you, Matt Malone," she said out loud, and felt sudden tears stinging her eyes. "Why couldn't you just have showed up when you said you would?" It was bad enough to be lost and alone, but it was a thousand times worse to feel so completely abandoned by a man she'd already come too close to giving her heart to. She stopped walking, caught between frustration, fear and anger, all of them connected with Matt.

If she hadn't stopped, she might not have heard the distant voice carried to her on the wind. She took in a startled breath, and then yelled "Hello!" at the top of her lungs. It had been a human voice, she was sure of it. Could she make enough noise, shouting against the wind, to be heard?

The answer was yes, and she laughed out loud in relief. What she heard was her own name, echoing through the winter air. It must be Matt calling to her, and his shouted "Lily!" was far sweeter than anything he'd said to her up till now.

"Matt!" she called back as loudly as she could, and heard him answer immediately. She started toward the sound, stopping now and then to shout again, and to try to pinpoint Matt's whereabouts by his voice. It was a ridiculous conversation—"Matt!" "Lily!"—but it was working. They were definitely getting closer together, and Lily picked up her pace. Before much longer she could hear him moving through the forest, pushing branches aside. Finally he came crashing past a stand of young spruce trees and stopped when he saw her.

Matt thought he'd never seen anything so beautiful. Her impossibly light blue eyes were open wide and glowing with

excitement. Did that mean she was glad to see him? Her
thick hair glistened slightly with melted snowflakes, and one
glance at her was enough to bring back to Matt's senses the
faint, flowery smell of her and the taste that had been
haunting him for weeks.

"Are you all right?" he asked, striding toward her. His
work boots rustled loudly in the leaves, and his red-and-
black plaid jacket made a bright splash of color in the
woods.

He'd been expecting a cool welcome, but instead, before
she'd said a word, Lily matched his own impatient strides
and closed the distance between them. He had her in his
arms almost before he realized it, and he was floored by the
eagerness he felt in the way she returned his embrace.

"Oh, Matt," she murmured, and held on even tighter.

Matt raised a hand to the face that was pressed into his
shirtfront and brushed away a trace of moisture on Lily's
cheek. It might have been a snowflake, or it might have been
something else—Matt didn't want to go into it now. For the
moment, it was more than enough just to hold her and know
that she wanted this closeness as much as he did. He didn't
understand it, but he didn't question gifts that had clearly
come straight from heaven.

It took a long while for Lily to get herself back in hand.
She was half-annoyed at her own response to seeing Matt.
Relief and desire had just boiled over together, and she'd
run straight into his arms without a second thought. Now
she was going to have to back off a little and reestablish the
distance between them, although she wasn't sure how to do
that when simply leaving his arms was this hard.

Still she made herself do it, and she made herself sound
as calm as she could when she answered his original question. "I'm fine," she said. "I just got a little turned around.
Did you come looking for me on principle, or did you figure I was lost?"

"I guessed you might be a little off the beaten track," he
said tactfully. "I keep meaning to blaze some proper trails

out here, but so far I just haven't had the time. I should have warned you how easy it is to get lost out here, but then I thought I'd be with you." He changed the subject abruptly. "You must be half-frozen. Did you find something worth painting, in spite of the weather?"

Lily held up her sketchbook. "A dozen paintings' worth," she said. "It really is beautiful here, Matt. I can see why you want to live here. But—"

She'd been starting to frame a polite excuse about wanting to get home before long, and he seemed to know it. "But you're cold, I know," he finished smoothly. "Fortunately, I lit a fire before I came looking for you. The place should be warm by the time we get back."

There was something in his face that kept Lily from pursuing the subject. He almost looked angry, and she wondered if he was mad at himself for spoiling what should have been a happy day together. For a moment Lily's willpower wavered. If he really felt bad about it . . .

Then she reminded herself that Matt's work had somehow managed to interrupt every encounter they'd ever had, and no amount of remorse was going to change that. When he put an arm around her shoulders, she couldn't resist the comforting warmth of his strong body, but she told herself firmly that she was not going to get roped into another scene where her emotions pulled her one way and her common sense another.

The cabin was surprisingly close by, but to reach it they had to climb over a steep, rocky ridge. "No fair putting bumps in the landscape like that," Lily said. "No wonder I got lost."

"Sorry," Matt said with a grin. "But if you want scenic panoramas, you've got to have a few bumps."

"I suppose." Lily swallowed, and her next words came out in a hurry. "Look, Matt, I was planning to be back home soon. I should be thinking about leaving."

He was still holding her close, and she could feel his muscles tighten around her. "You can't go until you've had lunch," he said firmly.

"I'm not hungry," she told him. "Besides, the snow is starting to build up. The roads will probably be worse later on."

"You're overlooking one thing," he said. Before she could react, he reached around with his free arm and pinned her even closer to his chest.

"What's that?"

"Before you can go anywhere, I have to let you go."

"That's true," she admitted. Her heart had been pounding since she'd seen him in the woods; now it was like a drumbeat in her ears.

"And I have no intention of letting you go if you're just going to run off on me."

"You mean you'd stand out here in the snow holding on to me, just to keep me from leaving?"

"No. I'd take you inside where it's warm, and hold on to you there. But you're not leaving until I've had a chance to make up for what I did to you this morning. And I've got a surprise for you, too. You wouldn't want to miss out on that, would you?"

"Bribery won't work. Now let me go, and we can talk about it." She moved against his arms, but his grip never loosened.

"Forget it. I've got you, woman, and you're not getting away from me yet."

"Matt, I'm serious. I won't be bullied."

"Don't think of it as bullying. Think of it as superior reasoning power."

"Aided by brute force."

"If you insist."

"What I insist is that you let me go. I'm a grown woman, and you can't—"

Matt didn't let her finish. As silently as the snowflakes all around them, he lowered his head and stopped her words with his lips. And as soon as she felt the hunger in his kiss, Lily knew why he was bullying her. It was sheer, unfulfilled need that was driving him.

"You hardly need to remind me that you're a grown woman," he said roughly, and then he kissed her again.

This time she couldn't keep from responding. He called to something deep inside her, called so insistently that his touch could mask all the perfectly sound reasons why she shouldn't be allowing herself to fall in love with this man. She opened her mouth to his strong, surging tongue and gave herself up to the delightful sensations of temporary insanity.

Their kiss seemed to feed on itself, growing in intensity until Lily lost track of where they were. Even the wet snowflakes landing on her cheeks had become a part of Matt's embrace surrounding her.

"God, Lily." He spoke with his lips against her thick hair. "I could kiss you for hours. And not just your lips—I want to kiss every inch of you."

Lily let her head fall back against his shoulder and gave a wordless moan as his lips found the soft skin at the base of her ear. He kissed her there so softly that she could feel all of her skin shivering ecstatically. How could any man be almost violently demanding one instant and unbelievably gentle the next?

"Let's go inside," he whispered, and she was helpless to do anything but nod silently in agreement.

Inside, the cabin was much more welcoming than when Lily had first entered it. There was a fire in the fireplace, and a large Persian rug had miraculously spread itself in front of it.

"Must be a magic carpet," Lily murmured. "It wasn't here earlier."

Matt smiled as he sat down next to her on the dark red carpet. "I bought it in Boston last week," he said. "Eventually it'll go in the master bedroom when the room is done. But for today, I figured it would do for a picnic blanket."

"Sounds like a pretty ritzy picnic," she commented, leaning back on her hands. "It'll really confuse the ants to have to cross a Persian carpet."

"I'm not expecting ants," he said. "A three-hour delay is enough of a setback for any picnic. Give me those shoes; they're soaked."

Deftly he removed both of her running shoes, setting them on the hearth to dry.

"Are you just trying to keep me from being able to make a quick getaway?" she asked.

"That's the idea," he said smoothly, sliding her socks off for good measure. "Anyway, these are wet. There's a bad cold going around these days, and we don't want you to catch it."

It was crazy to feel this much at home, Lily thought, sitting on a Persian carpet in her bare feet in an otherwise empty room. But she *did* feel at home, and she knew it was because of Matt.

"Thank you, Dr. Malone," she said, teasing gently. "And here I've been thinking you were a lawyer."

Instantly his face clouded. "No need to rub it in," he said. "As soon as I've fed you lunch, I'll give you a nice lawyerlike apology for standing you up this morning, and a binding contract not to do it again."

They ate Matt's picnic lunch in near silence, for which Lily was grateful. She had some hard thinking to do, and by the time they'd finished, she knew for certain that she didn't want to hear Matt's apology. Talking her into forgiving him would be a piece of cake for a glib speaker like Matt. She'd fallen into that trap before, forgiving and not quite forgetting over and over and over.

So when he repacked the picnic basket and turned to her with a purposeful look on his handsome face, she thought she was ready for him.

"Before you get all apologetic—" she started to say, but already he was one jump ahead of her.

"I know, I know," he said, holding his hands up, palms out. "You can't wait to see the surprise I told you about. Well, just sit tight." He got to his feet.

"That's not what I meant. Damn you, Matt Malone, why can't you ever let a person finish a single—"

"Tricks of the trade," he said, "as you ought to know." He was picking up something bulky that lay in the far corner of the room, and he had smiled back over his shoulder at her. "Keep the witness off guard."

"I'm not a witness. And I don't have ten years of courtroom experience behind me, so how am I supposed to know all the tricks of the trade?" she demanded.

The bulky object was wrapped in a blanket. Matt brought it back with him and sat next to Lily again.

"Good question," he said. He'd gotten exceedingly cocky again, for some reason. "As it happens, I think I have the answer. You're looking for a job, right?"

"Right." Lily's voice was cautious.

"And you don't want to work for some huge firm somewhere just to make money, right?"

"We've been through all this."

"Right. And I'm starting a new law practice."

She began to see where the cross-examination was leading. Matt twitched the corner of the blanket and unveiled the hidden object with a conjurer's flourish. Lily blinked once or twice, looking at an expensively gilded, hand-carved sign with two names on it—MALONE AND MARTI-NEAU. And underneath, carefully painted on was *Attorneys-at-Law*.

"Do you mean you want us to go into practice together?" Lily asked slowly.

"That's exactly what I mean." Matt got up again and propped the handsome sign against the stairway. "It makes all the sense in the world when you think about it. It's a great way for you to get some experience, and I've already had lots of inquiries from people who want to hire me once

I move here. If you sign on with me, we can split the work load and neither of us will have to work all the time."

"You mean you already know you're going to take on too much work," Lily muttered, but he went on in what she was sure was his best courtroom manner.

"I don't want you to think I'm trying to railroad you into a relationship," he said. "That's the last thing in my mind. But if we work together for a while, and things seem to be going in that direction, and if you come to realize that I'm not the workaholic I seem to be now—"

It was Lily's turn to interrupt. She put her hands over her ears, blocking his words. "Stop!" she said. "This is crazy. MALONE AND MARTINEAU can't ever happen, Matt. It should be MALONE *VERSUS* MARTINEAU, if it's anything."

Matt had clearly expected opposition. He rode right over her objections with a smile. "You're not thinking of all the advantages," he said. "I told you I was lucky enough to be taken under Derek's wing right at the beginning of my career. Well, nothing would satisfy me more than to be able to do the same thing for you—show you the ropes, steer you in whatever direction you want to go."

Lily got to her feet. She had to assert herself, and she did it by looking Matt right in the eye with a glare that finally seemed to get through to him.

"In the first place, I'm not asking anyone to take me under their wing—least of all, you," she said. "And you may have all this experience, but there's one area I know a lot more about than you do. Take my word for it, Matt, you and I can never be law partners, or any other kind of partners."

"I'm not talking about romance, I told you."

"You're a born lawyer, Malone. You can make anything sound convincing."

He frowned. "I mean what I say, Lily."

"With your mouth, or with your eyes? Because I'm getting some pretty mixed signals here." She was quickly putting her socks and shoes back on as she spoke. "What's the use pretending we aren't very, very attracted to each other? It's all very well to talk about having a nice platonic relationship as law partners and seeing where things lead, but you know where things would lead, as well as I do. And I—part of me wants that to happen. But I know it wouldn't work out in the end, and that's why I refuse to get into it."

"I told you I wouldn't push anything on you."

"But that's just what you're doing. You got this nice sign all carved before you ever said a word to me about your plan, and now you're refusing to take no for an answer."

His smile wasn't quite as robust as usual. "It's one of my best tactics," he said.

"I'm sure it is, but you're going to have to teach it—and all your other tricks—to some other willing young protégé, because I'm not the right woman for you."

She'd expected another onslaught of words, but he was uncharacteristically quiet. There was silence for a few seconds, and then Matt asked, still frowning, "If you're so sure you don't want anything to do with me, then why did you come today?"

Lily took a deep breath. She'd known they would have to get to this point. "I came because I wanted to see you again," she said simply, "and because I felt I should explain to you just why I'm so sure we're not right for each other."

She knew Matt well enough by now to realize that an argument was his natural response to anything that wasn't going his way. But now, for some reason, he just gestured to the red carpet and said, "Why don't you have a seat, and then we can talk."

They sat down on opposite ends of the big carpet. Neutral corners, Lily thought, and wished she could stop thinking of how this encounter might have turned out. Her imagination kept conjuring up scenes where she and Matt gave in to the passion they always awoke in each other. She kept picturing the two of them making love on the carpet, with the soft firelight flickering over them. It was an incredibly seductive image.

"Something wrong?" Matt asked, and Lily blinked to make the picture vanish.

"Yes, there is," she said, "and it's been wrong from the beginning. I probably should have told you about it then, but I never thought we'd get to be as...friendly as we are."

"Nice opening statement," he commented with a shadow of his usual humor. "Go on."

"What I should have told you is that for the past couple of years I was involved with another lawyer. He ran the firm where I worked one summer, and we sort of slid from working together into... other things."

She looked down at the convoluted patterns in the red carpet, not wanting to face Matt's eyes. "I was pretty idealistic, as you've pointed out more than once, and he was practicing the kind of law that appealed to me. We were planning to get married after I passed the bar, and work together in his firm."

"What went wrong?" Matt asked.

It was still easier to look at the carpet than at his face although she could feel the attraction of his body even from ten feet away. "Partly I started to realize that I wanted more from life than just a legal career. I told you I've always wanted a family of my own. Well, that started to seem more and more important to me, and I couldn't fit that in with the kind of life Alexander was leading."

"What kind of life was that?" Matt asked, although he must have had an inkling by now.

She looked up finally. "A typical lawyer's life," she said, and saw Matt wince. It gave her a kind of satisfaction. Now maybe he would start to understand.

She went on, explaining how all the little delays and frustrations had finally ruined what had been a happy relationship. Matt watched her with what seemed to be sympathy, as though he understood perfectly how she'd made the tough decision to break her engagement once she'd decided that marriage with Alexander would make both her home life and her career more difficult.

When she finished, Matt asked simply, "What finally ended things?"

Lily sighed. "He kept delaying our wedding, and after a while it just wore me down. We'd set the date, and then it would turn out to be inconvenient for his work schedule. The fourth time it happened, I told him if he couldn't take time off to get married, then maybe he shouldn't *be* married. He'd always been apologetic before about delaying and canceling things, but this time he told me I was asking for too much, and I wasn't going to get it from him. That was the end of it, just this past summer."

There was a long silence. A log settled in the fireplace, and Lily could hear sap oozing out of it and sizzling in the flames.

"Left some scars, I bet," Matt said finally.

"I'm not sure they're even scars yet," she admitted. "Still a bit too sore for that."

The silence grew. It was curiously peaceful now that she'd gotten her unpleasant story over with. She knew she should get up and go, but for some reason she waited.

Matt seemed as engrossed in the carpet pattern as she had been earlier. Then he spread his hands, palms up, a quirky smile on his face. "What can I say?" he asked. "I guessed there was something in your past that made you leery of workaholic lawyers, but I never imagined I was stepping right into somebody else's footsteps quite so neatly."

He shifted his position, and Lily watched him warily. She wished he would just admit defeat and make things easier for both of them. Unfortunately, she knew admitting defeat was not one of Matt's tricks of the trade.

"It isn't going to do you any good to argue, Matt," she began as he moved closer to her.

"Believe it or not, I wasn't going to argue. I'd say your case was locked up tight."

He was right beside her now, and she felt the familiar quivering deep inside that his nearness always caused. He'd shed his bulky jacket when they'd entered the house, and his deep green flannel shirt was open slightly at the neck. She could see a hint of copper-colored hair, and she longed to run her hands over the broad expanse of his chest.

"I'm glad you agree." She tried to sound as brusque as possible to counteract what she was feeling. "I really should get going, now—"

In one quick movement he'd surrounded her with one strong arm on each side of her body. "Not so fast," he said, his voice low. "I said I wasn't going to argue. I didn't say I wasn't going to persuade."

That was exactly what she didn't want. From the gleam in his eyes she could imagine what form of persuasion he was planning to use.

"That would be a bad idea, Matt," she said hastily, trying to stand up.

Her movement only brought their faces closer together. His lips were mere inches from hers as he said, "Can you really tell me you don't want to give us a chance?" he demanded, lowering his mouth to cover hers. In an instant, all the sweet, stabbing desire Lily had ever felt for this man came rushing back.

His lips were still grazing hers as he murmured, "And can you tell me this doesn't feel as good to you as it does to me?"

He lifted a hand and ran it upward along her torso until it found the firm circle of her breast. He claimed it with a master's touch, telling her he had a right to caress her like this.

She tried desperately to frame the words that would make him stop, but as he kneaded her soft flesh and found its hardened center even through the thickness of her sweater, a shuddering sigh was all the sound she was able to make.

His voice had sunk to a mere whisper, but every word seemed to warm and surround her. "I refuse to believe you," he said, "if you tell me you don't want things to go on from here." Impatient with the barrier of her cold-weather clothes, he put his hand inside the blue sweater and encountered the silkiness of her camisole. His fingertips glanced knowingly over her breasts, and she could hear the passion trembling in his breath. Then his hands slid lower, to the waistband of her jeans. Instinctively she arched her body toward those probing hands, wanting to take all the pleasure he could give her.

"Let me make love to you, Lily," he whispered, "and I guarantee you'll change your mind."

From another man, it might have sounded arrogant, but not from Matt. Lily knew already just how they would feel together—she'd been imagining it almost since the day they'd met. Matt could take her to new heights, show her things she'd barely even suspected were there.

And then what? The sobering thought finally managed to throw some cold water on Lily's escalating desire for him. The phone would probably ring, or afterward, Matt would get up and go back to work on some important case, and things would settle into the same pattern she'd just escaped from.

Oh, no, they wouldn't, because she wasn't giving them a chance to. She was sure that making love with Matt would be more physically fulfilling than anything she'd ever experienced, but emotionally it was a dead-end street. Therefore, she couldn't possibly make love with Matt. Thank goodness she had a tidy lawyerlike mind.

Things would have been easier if that tidy mind hadn't been harnessed to a treacherous body, which was clamoring for Matt's caresses. He ran a hand over her smooth, flat stomach and pulled her closer to him so that she could feel how ready he was to keep his promise to her. The image of their bodies entwining sensuously on the rich red carpet swam up in front of Lily's eyes again.

And again she fought it. It was just too dangerous to make love to Matt. If she let herself go that far, she'd be hooked. And removing hooks was too painful a process. With a struggle that was mental as well as physical, she wrenched herself free of his grasp and looked him in the eye.

"You can believe me or not," she said shakily. "But things aren't going any further between us, Matt, and no amount of persuasion is going to change my mind."

For the first time, Matt's frustration showed through. "You realize what you're doing, don't you?" he demanded, leaning back slightly. "You're cutting this off just because you're afraid of being hurt again."

"I prefer to think I'm just being sensible," she retorted. "I don't choose to get hurt twice in exactly the same way. I thought you'd understand."

"I understand why you were hurt so badly the first time. But that doesn't mean it's going to happen again."

Lily sighed. "It *has* happened, Matt! Beepers going off in my ear, dinners being interrupted, clients taking up your days off—how many more examples do I have to see?"

She stood up, mustering all the dignity she could. Matt was strangely silent, and it took all of her resolve to keep from looking back over her shoulder to see what he was doing. Trying to think up a rebuttal? Getting ready to come after her? Sitting there alone, his last ploy rejected?

The last picture was not a pleasant one. But she'd had to do what she'd done, Lily reminded herself as she gathered her sketching equipment and left the log house. Outside, the snow had almost stopped. The woods were dusted with white, and it looked as though the seasons had paused halfway between fall and winter. After the bright fire and Matt's embrace, it seemed desolate and depressing. Lily climbed into her car, still not looking back, and told herself she'd feel better when she got home.

Seven

"He called again," Sarah said as Lily walked in the apartment door and dropped her armload of groceries on the kitchen counter.

"Really? How many times does this make?"

Sarah consulted the little pieces of yellow notepaper stuck to the wall around their telephone. "Eight," she said. "And he doesn't sound like he's about to give up."

"No," Lily said a little grimly. "I can imagine that."

It had been more than a week since she'd seen Matt, and he'd been proving his persistence by calling her every day since then. She'd spent the long Thanksgiving weekend with Sarah at her parents' home in New Hampshire, but the change of scene hadn't helped her to stop thinking of Matt. And now she had come back to his daily messages on their answering machine. The fact that she didn't return his calls didn't seem to discourage him.

"Maybe you should call him back," Sarah suggested as she helped Lily put the groceries away.

"Getting tired of taking messages?" Lily grinned.

"Not at all. But I hope you bought more little notepads when you shopped, because at this rate we're going to run out pretty soon."

Lily's grin faded. "I just don't want to talk to him anymore, Sarah," she said tiredly. "We've said all we have to say."

"He doesn't seem to think so."

Lily felt a sudden flash of annoyance. "That man's problem is that he can't stand to admit defeat," she said. "He thinks he can talk anyone into anything."

"Well, he's good at it, judging by his reputation in the courtroom. And I know plenty of women who wouldn't mind being talked into spending time with Matt Malone," Sarah commented.

On her way to the refrigerator, Lily passed the growing field of yellow messages stuck to the wall, and stopped to reread them. "Call me at the office," the first one read, followed by Matt's business number. The second one was more to the point: "Call anytime, day or night." Wednesday's message had been a surprise: "In Vermont, chopping wood. Call me there." Chopping wood on a weekday? She'd been tempted to return that call, except she was sure it was just what he'd expected her to do.

He'd tried various other slants, from the ingenuous "Was it something I said?" to the imperious "Lily, call me. We need to talk." So far she'd held out against all of them, although yesterday's message had touched her in places she was trying very hard to keep sheltered. That note, in Sarah's sloping scrawl, had read, "Don't tell your roommate this, but I'm going crazy missing you."

She'd felt an undeniable ache when she'd read that. Suddenly it was harder to be calm and objective. In an instant she'd tasted all his kisses over again and felt the throbbing warmth of his body pulling her closer to him....

And kicked herself for letting those thoughts creep in. She'd been right to cool things down with Matt. Maybe, after he'd started his new life in Vermont, things could change, but that was a long way away. And *maybe* wasn't something she was pinning all her hopes on.

Today's message said simply, "Called again. Will continue to call," and Lily decided to ignore that one, too. She got out a chopping board and started to cook dinner, trying to think of other things.

A week later, Lily was sitting on the edge of her bed with the telephone in her hand. She was looking across the room to her dressing-table mirror, which had acquired the same symptoms as the kitchen wall. It was dotted with small yellow pieces of notepaper, all messages from Matt. After the first week, Sarah had started putting them in Lily's room. Lily sometimes suspected that her roommate was on Matt's side in this.

Maybe Sarah's strategy had worked, or maybe Matt's tenacity had worn Lily down. Or maybe it was the cryptic message he'd left on their answering machine today, and which Sarah had just stuck onto Lily's mirror. "You were right," it read. And that was all it said.

"Did he say right about what?" Lily had asked Sarah.

"No. Just 'You were right.'"

After a few minutes' thought, Lily dialed Matt's Boston number and was surprised when he answered on the first ring.

"Right about what?" she demanded without preamble.

"Ah." There was such satisfaction in his voice that Lily had to smile. "Ms. Martineau, I presume. Returning my call."

"Calls," she corrected him. "And what was I right about?"

She could hear him shift positions, and she couldn't keep from picturing the long, strong lines of his body. "You were right about me," he said simply. "About my being too committed to my career, I mean."

He paused, clearly expecting an answer, but Lily was too surprised to think of one. "Tell me more," she said finally.

"Well, I'll spare you all the heartrending details, but what it amounts to is that I've decided my nice open-ended offer about leaving Sloan and Baker gradually is for the birds. They'll keep giving me work to do as long as I'm around. The simple solution is for me just not to be around anymore."

"When are you leaving?" Lily asked.

"By the end of December, at the absolute latest."

"And then you'll be moving to Brattleboro?"

"You bet I will. The house is almost ready. I've got painters and carpet layers working overtime on it right now. And then—" Matt's voice changed suddenly, and Lily could hear how important this was to him "—then you'll change your mind about me."

"Is that an order, Mr. Malone?"

"No, just a prediction. That's the good news. The bad news is that in the meantime, I'm literally snowed under with work, trying to get things ready to pass along to new people. And I know that sounds like a crummy excuse for calling you instead of driving down to see you, but believe me, Lily, in another month I'll never have to make excuses again."

"And I know *this* sounds like a crummy excuse, but I've heard that one before." Lily could feel her resolve melting, but she forced herself to stay objective. Matt's promises were tempting, but they were still nothing but words.

"Well, after this month you'll never have to hear it again. Which brings up another subject—what are you doing for Christmas?"

"One of my cousins is getting married. I'm going out to California for the wedding."

"New Year's?"

"I won't be getting back until the day after New Year's."

"Well, it was a good try. But by the time you get back, I'll be officially moved to Vermont. So you have to come and visit."

Lily gave up her attempt to be cool and objective. "Oh, Matt, I'd love to come and visit, but—"

"Hold it right there," he ordered her as though he didn't want to hear what came next. "No more 'buts.' "

"This is an important one," she insisted. "Part of me really does want to see you again, Matt, but I still have a lot of reservations, and most of them have to do with believing promises before I've seen that they're true."

"There's a word for that, you know," he said soberly. "Some people call it *trust*."

"I've heard of it," Lily said, "but my experience with it hasn't been very good."

There was a long pause, and then Matt asked, "So what are you trying to tell me?"

"Just that I need some more time to sort out how I feel and to see how things change for you once you've moved. Then maybe we can pick up where we left off."

"How long will that take?"

"I don't know. Why don't we say we'll meet again at our court appearance?"

"Lily, that's not until March!" he exploded.

"It's only four months, Matt."

"*Only* four—" He sounded as though he'd bitten off the rest of the sentence. She wished she could see his expression; it was hard to tell just what was going on in that razor-sharp mind. When he spoke again, he sounded calmer, and that made her suspicious. "So you don't want to meet again until the trial, huh?"

"That's right." Why was he being so docile all of a sudden?

"All right, I guess I can handle that. I think our defense is pretty well settled, don't you?"

"I'd say so." He really had her wondering now.

"Then I guess I'll see you in court."

Lily hung up feeling that Matt had somehow gained the upper hand, and she had no idea how or why.

She found out before long. The nice, safe four-month buffer she'd counted on vanished into the air when she received notice that their court appearance, originally intended for late March, had been moved up to mid-January. She'd read the letter in surprise, then smiled in spite of herself.

"You get an A for effort on this one, Mr. Malone," she'd said out loud to no one in particular.

The tan Lily must have acquired in California over Christmas hadn't begun to wear off by the time Matt saw her walk through the front door of the courthouse, squinting slightly as she stepped out of the bright January sunshine. He felt his heart start to pound as he caught sight of her slim figure coming toward him. Her heart-shaped face was as beautiful and provocative as ever, and her eyes as wide and blue. She was wearing a black sweater and a wool suit of a deep, glowing red that reminded him of the Persian rug at his cabin, now on the floor of his new master bedroom. He'd had such improbable plans when he'd first brought that carpet to Vermont, hoping against hope that Lily would trust him enough to make love with him on its lush surface. He'd wanted her to see it as an oasis of comfort amid the bareness of his new house.

He didn't know if he could really persuade Lily to give him another chance. He didn't know if she'd had enough time to get over the pain of her broken engagement. The only thing he knew for certain was that Lily Martineau was the woman he'd been waiting for all his life, and he couldn't dream of letting her go.

There was a glint of humor in her eyes as she approached him. "Excuse me," she said in an exaggerated, polite manner, "but I'd like some advice."

They fell into step together as they started toward the courtroom.

Matt raised his eyebrows. "Advice about what?" he asked.

"Well, I'm thinking of becoming a high-powered corporate lawyer, and I was wondering if you could tell me what some of the fringe benefits are."

"Fringe benefits?"

"Yes. I mean, if I were a well-known corporate lawyer, would I be able to pull enough strings to get a trial date moved up two months?"

"Oh, I see." Was she reminding him again of the gulf between her legal world and his? "Offhand, I'd say it would be possible, if you were quite insistent and knew a lot of people."

"I thought so."

They reached the courtroom and stopped outside the door. He could sense her deliberately holding him at arm's length, and it was driving him crazy. The hidden meaning in her lighthearted words was only too obvious. He'd managed to get their trial date changed, but to her it was only one more proof that he was completely involved in his job.

"It was either get the trial date changed or come to Hartford and carry you off bodily," he informed her gruffly, taking her small chin in one hand and drinking in the sweet perfume of her hair and skin. "And somehow I didn't think you'd respond well to that."

"Matt, if you could just try to believe me when I tell you—"

She never got to the end of the sentence. The look on Matt's face stopped her short just before his lips covered hers. With a complete disregard for the people passing them in the corridor, he pulled her close to him, and she could feel the desire in his very bones.

Everything inside her answered him wildly. The memories that had kept her company every night for the past weeks had been just pale reminders of what his touch was like, and she knew as their mouths merged for one glorious, passion-crowded instant that she was just as much in danger of falling in love with Matt Malone as she'd ever been. The weeks of being apart had only made this moment more unbearably seductive.

His tongue curled around hers in a lavish embrace. She took in a long breath that was filled with the scent of him, clean and enticingly masculine. She was a fine one to accuse Matt of sending mixed signals, she thought disjointedly. Her words had always said no to Matt, but physically, whenever he touched her, she told him yes from head to toe.

And then, in another instant the world tilted upright again, and the courthouse corridor came back into focus. People still went purposefully about their business, heels clicking on the marble floor. Everything was the same except the inner world of Lily Martineau.

Matt, too, looked shaken and completely unlike the poised, businesslike attorney he'd been ten minutes ago. His eyes were unusually dark and soft. "I was just checking," he said, "to see if things were still the same between us."

"I—I'm afraid they are, Matt. We're still attracted to each other, and I'm still not convinced it can work." It was an effort to speak calmly, or at all.

"I'll believe you," he said fiercely, "when you stop kissing me back as though you meant it. Shall we go in now?"

Lily had to admit he had a talent for getting to the punch line first, although she wished he wouldn't use it quite so often. She walked ahead of him into the courtroom, thinking of how she'd always enjoyed the solemn atmosphere of a court of law. It was a place where things happened in their proper order at a deliberate pace. She'd found that appealing and calming.

But there was nothing calming about it today. She felt as though she were sitting next to a volcano, in the person of Matt Malone. He might stay dormant, or he might explode without warning—there was no way to be sure.

Thomasina Thompson was already there, sitting beside her lawyer and looking in much better shape than when they'd last seen her. In fact, something about her seemed to suggest that she was actually enjoying being there. Once again Lily had an odd flash of sympathy for the old woman. Elderly, handicapped and frail, she could easily spend her life being overlooked. Instead she seemed to manage to make herself the center of attention. It was quite an accomplishment, Lily had to admit.

Of course, she could see Matt's point of view, too, and no doubt his was more reasonable. Tommy's lawsuit was unnecessary and expensive, and the courts were busy enough as it was. But still Lily had to applaud the old woman's spirit. If you let things roll over you, you get flattened, she thought, and obviously Tommy had no intention of letting that happen.

As she took her seat beside Matt, Lily wondered why this unexpected admiration for Tommy kept cropping up. Was it because ever since her parents died, she'd had the same sense that she had to rely on herself to make her way in the world? Other people—aunts, cousins, teachers— hadn't really helped, and Alexander had been a definite hindrance. Twenty-six years of life had left her with the conviction that she herself was the only person she could really count on.

All the more reason to keep Matt Malone at arm's length then. She remembered the way he'd insisted that they go into business together and thought that he would probably be only too glad to take charge of her life for her. Lily sat up very straight in her chair, smoothing the dark red fabric of her skirt over her knees.

"We're sticking to the same strategy?" she asked him as he pulled file folders out of his expensive and slightly battered briefcase.

"Absolutely." He sounded confident and calm, and she felt very much like the junior member of the team. It was Matt's show now. He'd suggested that he should do all the speaking since he was far more experienced in the courtroom, and the part of Lily that was worried about winning this case had agreed that he was right. But there was also the part that wanted her to start building her own experience, that felt overshadowed by Matt's brilliant reputation and that resented the way Matt had taken control of things. Second fiddle, she thought. *Again.*

The opening statements were brief and to the point. Tommy's lawyer stressed the mental and physical suffering his client had gone through. Matt didn't deny the suffering but stated that the accident had been Tommy's own fault, and that he and Lily would call witnesses to prove it.

The calling of those witnesses proved to be a much longer process than anyone had anticipated, Matt included. Back in November he and Lily had lined up half a dozen people willing to come into court to say that they had seen Tommy pull away from Lily's grip and stagger backward into the path of Matt's Jeep. But Tommy's lawyer insisted on cross-examining each witness. His strategy was to show that there were two possible interpretations to what had happened, and the questioning and counter-questioning took a great deal of time.

"Do we really need all these witnesses after all?" Lily asked Matt as he sat down after one round of questions. "It seems as though we're using a sledgehammer to crush a walnut. We could make the same point without all the fuss."

"I disagree," Matt said firmly. "I've seen cases like this come down to a matter of you-did-I-didn't. I don't want to take a chance on that happening, so yes, we do need all these witnesses."

He was reminding her again, Lily thought, that he had experience and she had none. And there was no doubt that he was very good at commanding a courtroom. He had a way of speaking that seemed to include everyone in the back row, and his simple, down-to-earth approach was much more effective than another lawyer's arm-waving histrionics could have been. Knowing Matt's reputation, Lily had expected him to be more heavy-handed and dramatic in the courtroom, but now she realized that his direct, conversational style was very, very effective.

Unfortunately, as the afternoon wore on, it became clear that Tommy Thompson was a trickier opponent than they'd thought. She hadn't said a word out loud, but her appearance—from her battered felt hat to the white cane in her gnarled old hands—spoke loudly in her own defense. Lily could see the jury members looking from Matt's impressive form to the table where Tommy sat and could almost hear the questions in their minds. Was this a case of two sharp lawyers ganging up on a helpless old woman?

Matt had noticed the same thing. The next time there was a lull in the proceedings, he whispered to Lily, "I don't like this poor-little-old-me act. What happened to the scrappy Tommy Thompson we all knew and loved?"

"I know," Lily whispered back. "I'd been counting on her to get up and yell at us, so everyone would see what she's really like. If she just keeps sitting there and looking pitiful, I'm going to get worried."

Sitting and looking pitiful did seem to be Tommy's strong suit, and although Lily was sure it was an act, she had to admit it was a good one. From time to time Tommy asked her lawyer a question in a soft undertone—a far cry from the strident tones Lily had heard at their ill-fated first meeting—and whenever she did, she reached out for her lawyer's hand as though seeking reassurance. It was a moving gesture, and the jury didn't miss it.

"She should have been an actress," Matt muttered. "Well, here goes." And he got to his feet to examine another witness.

Matt was building their case on facts alone, asking his witnesses simply to describe what they'd seen. Lily could tell he was saving his own interpretation of the facts until the end. It was a sound, reasonable line of defense to take, she knew.

But Tommy's lawyer was using his client's age and appearance to fullest advantage, and against Tommy's seeming helplessness, Matt's strategy of sticking strictly to the facts wasn't as effective as it should have been. The next time he sat down beside her, she could sense the tension beneath his professional calm. "Don't look now," he said, leaning over so that his lips almost grazed her hair, "but the big clock on the wall says we're running out of time."

Lily glanced at her watch. There wouldn't be enough time left in today's court session to call their remaining two witnesses, and they still had to hear Lily's and Tommy's own testimony.

"That means another day of this, I guess," she said.

"Right. His honor's just about to break the bad news."

The judge was rising, and the rest of the court with him. The announcement was made that the trial would continue first thing on Monday morning, and Lily heard an outright groan from one of the remaining two witnesses, who had been watching the clock anxiously.

She was tempted to add her groan to his. Missing work on Monday wasn't a problem—she was able to set her own schedule at the insurance company—but the thought of driving back to Hartford for the weekend, and then back to Boston early on Monday didn't appeal to her at all. She'd wanted to get all this over with as quickly as she could. Just being near Matt was stirring up all kinds of things she didn't feel ready to deal with.

At the moment, he seemed to be feeling nothing but ir-
ritation at the way the trial had gone. "Looks like we've
got some more work to do," he said brusquely as he shuf-
fled papers back into his briefcase.

"Good thing you don't mind working on weekends,"
Lily said. She could see where this was headed, and she had
no intention of getting into any more get-togethers with
Matt.

"Too bad you *do* mind it," he countered. "Shall we eat
dinner first, or hit the law library right away?"

Lily took a deep breath and reminded herself of all the
resolutions she'd made about this man. "In the first
place," she said, "if you want my professional opinion,
'hitting the law library' is not the way to approach this
case. In the second place, I have a perfectly good dinner
waiting for me in my refrigerator in Hartford. And in the
third place—" she looked him straight in the eye "—if you
want to do any more work on this, you'll be doing it on
your own."

Now that their eyes had locked, Lily was finding it difficult to look away again. Matt was frowning slightly, and
his dark brown eyes were utterly serious.

"You're not playing by the rules," he informed her.

"I'm not?"

"No. You just expressed a professional opinion on this
case, and then you tell me to handle it on my own."

"That was your decision," she said. "Since you have all
the experience and I have none—"

"You sound as though you resent that."

"No, it's not that. It's just—" How could she make it
clear to him? "I understand that you're the best one to
take charge of this case. It's just I feel like a sidekick, or a
mascot or something. I've felt like that all my life, Matt,
and I'm getting pretty tired of it."

Matt stopped short, cutting off whatever he had been
going to say. He'd insisted on handling their defense because he wanted to be sure they won, but it had never oc-

curred to him that in winning the case he might lose more
points with Lily. He'd understood how her empty childhood had affected her and how her experience with Alexander had made her leery of overpowering, work-driven
lawyers. But until now he'd never really felt just how
strong her need for independence was. He could see it in
the line of her lips and the steady gaze of her eyes. And it
only made him want her more.

He half leaned, half sat on the edge of the table, one leg
swinging carelessly above the floor. The courtroom was
almost empty now. "If you're so sure my strategy is
wrong," he said, "what do you suggest we replace it
with?"

"I was thinking of a more...personal approach," she
said. "Not so many facts."

Matt frowned. "I don't like that kind of defense," he
said. "If you don't stick to the facts, you end up with a
decision based on what the jury members think of your
personality, and if they like the tie you're wearing."

Lily hesitated. She was wavering inside between the desire to stay clear of entangling herself with Matt Malone,
and the unexpected challenge she was feeling. She *could* do
a good job with their defense, she was sure. She might be
inexperienced, but she understood some things about human nature.

"Well, look what's happening now," she said. "We're
presenting all the facts, and Tommy's scoring points just
by looking old and pitiful. I think we should try to counter that by a little personality of our own."

"That could be very tricky."

"It could also win us this case."

"It'll take some extra work. We'll have to rethink what
to do with those last two witnesses on Monday."

"I suppose," Lily said slowly, "that I wouldn't mind
putting in some extra work."

Was she being an utter fool? All she could think of was
that this was the first real professional challenge she'd had,

and it felt good to have a real, meaty legal bone to worry at.

That didn't mean she was giving up her whole weekend. "I think we can wrap this up over dinner," she said to Matt. "There's no need for me to stay in Boston."

Matt snapped his briefcase shut. Lily looked at his strong fingers working the brass catches and thought that the snap of the leather case closing sounded harsh in the now-empty courtroom. She waited for Matt to answer, and when he finally looked up at her, his face was strangely guarded.

"How's your broken heart doing these days?" he asked, looking carefully into her face.

The unexpected question made Lily laugh. "Speaking of non sequiturs," she said, but Matt pressed the point.

"I'm serious," he said, and he looked it. His thick auburn brows were drawn together over his dark eyes. "I've been wondering a lot if you'd gotten any less bitter about your engagement falling apart."

"I guess I sounded pretty bitter last fall."

"Understandably, I would say."

"If you're trying to get me to say I've softened my views on lawyers who spend all the time working—"

"I'm not trying to get you to say anything at all. I just asked you a simple question."

And he seemed prepared to wait for the answer. "Well, if you really want to know, it's not nearly so painful to think about it now. It's been long enough that I think I've finally gotten some perspective on the whole business."

"That's good. Now, Ms. Martineau—" he lapsed into the courtroom manner she'd seen him using all afternoon "—would it be fair to say you've softened your views on lawyers who spend all the time working?" There was a smile glinting in his eyes.

"Forget it, Matt. I'm not biting."

"Well, I had to try. But Lily, listen to me. There's something I want to say to you, and I'm having a hard time working up to it."

"If it's about us—"

"Let's just say, for the moment, that it's about me."

Lily crossed her arms, waiting for him to explain.

"This week I'm going to be wrapping up my final case for Sloan and Baker. On Monday afternoon, as a matter of fact."

"I thought you said you were finishing up at the end of December, no matter what."

"Well, I tried, but this one ruling got delayed."

Clearly he was trying to gloss over the delay. Both of them were aware of other delays and other excuses in the past, but for the moment they didn't pursue the subject.

"Anyway, after that case I'm off to Brattleboro for good. So the Matt Malone you've been objecting to is officially changing his stripes after Monday afternoon. And I'm asking you to give the new, improved Matt Malone a chance to prove he's the man you're really looking for."

"Matt, people don't just change their personalities in a single afternoon! You've been bound up in your career because of the way you are—ambitious, fond of arguing, good at fighting, all those things. You may think you're going to change, but I predict you'll end up with the same kind of career in Brattleboro that you have now in Boston."

"Good at looking into the future, aren't you?"

"Sometimes, I think I am." She held her ground firmly.

"So you don't believe people can ever change?"

"Some kinds of change, yes. But Alexander was always telling me he was going to take more time off, too, and it never happened."

"I'm not Alexander," Matt said through clenched teeth. "Maybe I should have pointed that out before now."

"In a lot of important ways, you're very much like him."

"In a lot of ways, I think you've been looking at me through Alexander-colored glasses," he shot back. "All the little things that have gone wrong between you and me have just gotten added on to Alexander's account in your mind. And now I don't get another chance just because Alexander didn't deserve one."

Lily hesitated. Had she been doing that?

Matt went on in a gentler tone of voice. "That's why I asked you if you thought you'd gotten over things a little more now. I know you've been hurt, and hurt badly. But I think it's time you stopped protecting your feelings blindly and took a chance on falling in love with someone again."

She felt her own instinctive reaction—"I don't want to fall in love again"—and wondered again if he might be right. She'd always been independent and protective of her deepest feelings. Maybe, after her failed engagement, she'd allowed too thick a skin to grow over them.

The courtroom setting made it easy to conjure up Alexander's image. He'd been slim and sleek, quite a contrast to Matt's robust good looks, his strong, broad chest, his honest, piercing brown eyes. There was the same strength of purpose in both of them, and maybe that was why Matt had made her so wary at first. But Alexander had never been as patiently understanding as Matt was being now. It was an important difference.

Maybe Matt was right. Maybe it was time to take a chance on loving again.

It was like standing at the edge of a cold pool, daring herself to dive in. She couldn't do it quite yet. "I'm not about to make a hundred-and-eighty-degree change in my opinion of you, you know," she told Matt.

Her mouth was prim again, Matt noticed, a sure sign of something going on inside her.

"That's fine." He sensed her careful capitulation and was quick to take her up on it. "I'm not asking you to do that."

"Then what, specifically, *are* you asking me?"

He chose his words as carefully as he'd ever done in a court of law, knowing he could tip Lily one way or the other. "I'm asking that you not make any more judgments about me until you've seen me in my new situation in Vermont. I'm asking that you pretend, for now, that we're starting from scratch, without any beepers or interruptions or telephones ringing at dinner. And—" Matt drew a deep breath because it was hard to say in words what he was longing to express with his whole body "—I'm asking that you stay with me this weekend, Lily. Not to work, but just to, well, shall we say, explore some possibilities?"

"You mean stay with you at your apartment?"

"That's exactly what I mean." His voice was a growl, and Lily clearly saw the depth of his desire in his eyes.

She was so drawn to him that it was hard to think rationally. The cautious side of her insisted that she throw in a condition or two, though. "I'm not committing myself to anything," she told him. "If I stay, it's only for this weekend, and I'll have to wait and see whether or not things really change once you get to Brattleboro."

"Fair enough," he said quickly. She was so close to saying yes at last, and it took every ounce of his willpower to keep from wrapping her in his arms then and there.

"And I don't want to talk about whether or not we have a future," she said. "It's too soon for that." Matt could see that her breathing, like his own, was quickening in spite of the politeness of their conversation.

"Fine by me," he said, and suddenly he couldn't keep from touching her for a moment longer. He pushed himself away from the table and pulled her to him with one arm. "Come home with me now, Lily." His voice was roughened by passion, and he saw it mirrored in those light blue eyes. "And I'll start to prove to you that we can be whatever you want us to be."

Eight

Lily didn't pay much attention to the walk back to Matt's apartment. Physically she was stepping along through the brisk cold of the early January evening, but her imagination had already raced ahead, and she was only dimly aware of the streets and buildings surrounding her.

Matt seemed to share her mood. He kept one arm tightly around her shoulders, and from time to time she could feel his fingers squeezing her even through her coat, as though he was double-checking that she really was there and not just some figment of his imagination. She had to walk quickly to match his long strides, but she didn't feel rushed. She felt as if she were being borne along on a benevolent wave. She had no idea where it was taking her, but for the moment she was content just to ride it wherever it was going.

They climbed the narrow staircase in his building with their arms still around each other, and they only barely fit. Lily laughed. "I think it would be safe to let go of me now," she said as her shoulder wedged against the wall.

Matt only held her tighter. "Forget it," he said. "I'm not taking a chance on having you walk out on me again."

Lily paused and looked at him. The light in the hallway was dim, and Matt's usually piercing brown eyes seemed almost liquid. He was watching her with a hunger that was as arousing as his touch.

"For this weekend," she said, "I promise I won't walk out on you."

"Just for this weekend." He echoed her words.

"Yes," she said. "Beyond that, I'm not promising anything at all, remember."

"I remember," he said. He didn't push her any further. Instead he took her hand in his and pulled the leather glove from it slowly. Then he pressed his lips to the center of her palm, a gentle gesture that somehow made Lily's blood race. It was a potent reminder of how drawn to each other they were, when the simple touch of his mouth could turn her bones to water.

"Oh, Matt," she said without meaning to, and felt his frame shudder in response.

For an instant he pulled her closer to him, burying his face in her hair. Then he growled, "Let's go inside. The building management is very specific about not allowing any ravishment in the hallways." Lily laughed in spite of her wildly pounding heart and followed him into his apartment.

She had wondered if there would be an awkward moment when they finally faced each other alone, but to her surprise, there was none at all. She welcomed the sound of Matt closing the door behind them, knowing that she was doing something she had been wanting to do for a long, long time.

"Allow me to take your wrap," Matt said, his customary grin finding its way through the tension obvious in his face. He threw their coats over the back of a chair and then turned to the fireplace. The night was damp and the unused apartment chilly, but before long Matt had laid a wood fire in the grate. The sound of kindling catching hold seemed to bring a new warmth to the room.

"There," he said, standing up with an air of finality. "That's enough of being the perfect host."

Lily had been standing by the sofa, watching his strong hands stack the firewood and hold the match to the dry tinder. She was half smiling at the absurd notion that he had already done that to her—kindled something that was slowly taking hold of her entire body—when he turned to look at her.

"Why the smile?" he asked. His own face was serious.

Lily didn't want to explain her fanciful thoughts. She settled for saying, "I was just thinking about you."

Her smile deepened until Matt saw her seldom-seen dimple appear in one cheek.

Matt caught his breath at the look on Lily's face. He had never seen her so open or so yielding. Finally he'd managed to vanquish that polite smile. It made the three months of waiting more than worthwhile.

For a long moment he didn't move but just caressed her with his eyes. He couldn't quite believe she was here or that she'd agreed to spend the weekend with him. He had a notion that Lily might simply vanish on him even now. The deep sable color of her hair and the way her deep red suit seemed to merge with the muted reds of his Persian carpet made her seem like something out of a dream.

He stepped toward her and slowly slid his arms around her. She was no dream but flesh and blood, and just as breathless as he was. He could feel her heart beating against his chest and heard her sharp intake of breath as his hand followed the long curve of her thigh.

"You make me feel so alive," she murmured.

There was a note of triumph in Matt's low chuckle. "This is only the beginning, my love," he promised her.

The fire was beginning to crackle animatedly now, its light spilling into the dimly lit room. Matt had switched on a stained-glass table lamp when they'd arrived, but aside from those two pools of warm light, everything was half in darkness. It was as if they were in an enchanted cave, Lily thought.

She took off her red wool jacket, hearing the satin lining hiss as she dropped it over the end table. There was still no sense of awkwardness or hesitation. Making love to Matt seemed to be the most natural thing in the world. She wasn't even really thinking of making love, just of following her feelings to wherever they led.

Matt took off his jacket and tie and was starting to reclaim her in his arms when she said, "Wait." She reached out to his crisp white shirtfront, amazed at her own boldness, and began unbuttoning it.

The look on his face made her blood surge wildly through her veins. Suddenly she wanted to see all of him. The strength in his body had been an excitement and a torment in all the weeks she hadn't seen him but had thought of him inescapably. Now she wanted more. She wanted to know how he felt and how he would respond when she touched him.

Her fingers trembled as she undid the last button and slid the shirt from his shoulders. Naked, his upper body was even harder and more muscular than she'd thought. His shoulders were powerful. She outlined them with her hands and heard a groan from deep in Matt's throat. A light dusting of curly auburn hair covered his chest, which was obviously in fighting trim.

"Oh, God, Lily." Another low groan escaped him. "You don't know what that does to me."

She had a fairly good idea, because it was doing the same thing to her. She let Matt pull her closer at last and felt the springy bare flesh of his back with both hands. He was just as gorgeous and just as vital as she'd thought in her half admitted daydreams.

Her body was humming with an abandoned passion she couldn't remember ever feeling before. She could feel the pressure of his own throbbing desire, and her breath came a little faster. How had she ever held out against something that inflamed her this way?

He was kissing her now, his lips hungry and gentle at the same time, and sliding one hand under the edge of her black cashmere sweater to caress the soft flesh beneath. "I want to see all of you," he said without taking his lips from hers. "I want to know how beautiful you are."

Lily leaned back in his embrace and pulled the sweater over her hair. It fell to the floor by her feet and was joined in an instant by the silky white camisole she'd been wearing. Perhaps the fire had warmed the room already, because she had no sensation of cold. Or maybe it was Matt's eyes that heated her, or the blanket of his breath as he bent his head to kiss the smooth flesh at her collarbone.

He reached behind her back and in one movement unsnapped her bra and pulled it free. Her full, firm breasts were already arched toward him as if asking for his touch, and when he cradled them in his hands, Lily gasped out loud with delight. His thumbs caressed their smoothness, and she could picture the brown strength of his hands traveling over the whiteness of her skin. Then he moved on to the buttons at the waistband of her skirt.

Lily had never had a man undress her before, and it was strangely exciting to stand trembling while Matt stripped away the clothes that covered her. She could feel his own excitement and his sense of delight in what he was discovering. When she finally stood naked in his arms and felt his knowing hands touching off cascades of feeling in places deep inside her, she nearly laughed out loud with pleasure.

"Your skin is so beautiful," Matt told her, and ran his hands lightly from her thigh to her shoulder to prove it to her. "It's like a perfect snowdrift with the light from the setting sun shining on it."

Lily could almost feel the firelight flickering over her skin as Matt spoke. His voice was quiet and rough with the desire he still held in check.

Quickly he rid himself of the rest of his clothes. There was a long, heart-stopping moment while he gazed into Lily's soul, seeming to question her. Yes, her eyes told him silently. *Yes.*

Then he moved toward her, and the sensation of their bodies meeting with no barrier between them was like a new awakening for her. They were shaken by the same long, shuddering breath, and Lily could tell that the self-control Matt was fighting so hard for was in danger of snapping. His hardened flesh pressed against her with an insistence that her body begged to answer.

"The sofa," Matt murmured, "is closer than the bed." He kept his arms around her as they settled into the burgundy depths of the sofa. "You're smiling again," he said, looking down at her face.

"I can't help it," she replied. And then words were swept away by the force of their longing for each other, and Matt kissed her with a savage intensity that Lily astonished herself by matching. Every part of her was aching for him, demanding what she knew he could give her. Never before had she felt herself such an equal partner. There was no one in command here, just a man and a woman driving each other to a higher and higher pitch by their own desire.

Matt seemed determined to spin out the exquisite agony as long as he could. His lips moved to the base of her neck and then lower to her breasts. His tongue grazed the hardened center and then went on to ring the soft flesh with kisses that were half breath, half caress. Lily moaned at their lightness, intently aware of the charged silence in the room and the way her nerves leaped like a flame wherever Matt's touch lighted.

For an instant his face was hidden between her breasts, and she ran her fingers through his thick auburn hair. She could feel the excitement vibrating through him, and it built up her own. Part of her wanted to feel him inside her now, and the rest of her wanted to know where his next caress would lead.

•

He slid his hands over her smooth, flat stomach and around to grasp the roundness of her bottom. She might have been moulded to fit in that gentle grip, she thought, and then caught her breath in delight as his mouth, too, slid downward. For the briefest, most devastating moment, his tongue found the place that could give her a pleasure beyond words. Lily gave a sharp-edged cry, and then the searing sensation was gone as Matt turned his face to kiss the silken skin of her inner thigh.

Maybe Matt could keep up this slow and deliberate pace forever, but Lily's control was long gone. The warmth of his breath had seemed to shoot to the very center of her being, and her voice was almost a sob as she said, "Please, Matt. Love me now." She had never felt so demanding and so yielding at the same time as she raised her arms and pulled him back toward her.

There was a long, slow smile on Matt's face. "That's what I've been waiting to hear," he said, and Lily had no strength left to resent his look of triumph. She needed him now as she'd never needed any man before.

She raised herself to meet him, and gave another wordless cry as he buried himself within her. It felt so right that Matt Malone should be the one to touch and fill and satisfy the empty places deep inside. She moved in a slow rhythm that he instinctively followed, and now it was she who was maddening Matt. She couldn't think of prolonging the pleasure; all she wanted was to propel herself toward the point that had been beckoning to her, first vaguely and now so insistently, ever since she'd met Matt. Her mind was free of all thoughts but that.

Matt was caught up now in the pulsating drive. He gave up all his notions of holding back and making this last, and thrust deeper and deeper into her. He was aware that he was holding her with a strength that might be painful, but he was powerless to do anything about it. The only thing that mattered was the overwhelming sensation of being driven to this mutual goal. He'd been dreaming of making love with Lily

Martineau for three months, but this unimaginable need
went eons beyond anything he'd expected.

For a moment it seemed as though the rhythm of their
moving together could go on forever. And the next moment, on the same breath, both of them cried out as everything seemed to shudder and move in a convulsive explosion
that came from somewhere inside. The urgency of that
movement went on and on, and finally, gradually, it resolved itself into an aftermath of sweetness that left them
both silent, drained and astonished by the power of what
they had felt.

Finally Matt stirred, and she could see his profile in the
soft firelight. The corners of his mouth were tilted in that
now-familiar grin.

"I haven't made love on a sofa since I was in high
school," he said lazily.

"You must have gone to a very advanced high school,"
Lily commented just as dreamily.

"Let's just say I was a quick learner," he told her, and the
grin gave way to something more serious. "But in all those
years, Lily, I've never felt anything quite like that."

Lily reached a hand up to his face and ran her fingers
down the strong line of his cheekbone. She had to admit to
herself that she'd never felt anything quite like this, either,
not the compelling drive and this sweet sense of completeness.

That thought was a double-edged sword, but she found
reassurance in knowing she'd made no lasting commitments beyond this weekend. No doubt that was why their
lovemaking had been so supremely successful. There were
no strings attached, and she could let herself go without
thoughts of what came next.

Matt stood up and walked to an antique wooden blanket
box that sat next to the fireplace. He pulled a heavy quilt
from its depths and said, "In a moment I'm going to go
back to being the perfect host, and go get us something to
drink. But I want to hold you for just a while longer first."

Lily couldn't imagine moving, especially after Matt had covered them both with the quilt and settled back into the corner of the sofa with Lily in his arms. Her head was leaning against his chest, and she could hear his heartbeat gradually slowing. It was a comforting sound, and half-mesmerizing.

"I don't need a drink," she said sleepily. "I'd rather lie here with you."

He pulled her a little closer, and she felt him kissing her through the thickness of her tousled hair. She tilted her face toward his, her eyes closed, and their lips met with a new familiarity that stirred them both all over again. There was passion flickering between them still, but it was a gentle thing now and not so demanding. It promised even better things to come, Lily thought as she settled back into the curve of Matt's arm with a contented sigh. After all, they had the whole weekend ahead of them.

The steady crackling of the fire and the rhythm of Matt's breathing were like soft pillows for Lily to lean back on. She tried to open her eyes, found them too heavy and gave up trying. Thoughts of making love with Matt were still drifting hazily through her mind as she fell asleep.

It was dark, and there was nothing left in the grate but glowing embers the next time Lily opened her eyes. They were lying as they'd been when they'd both fallen asleep, with Matt in the corner of the wide sofa and Lily tucked against his side.

He was still asleep, she realized, and she couldn't resist the temptation to touch him while he was unaware of her. She ran her hand over the expanse of his chest, feeling the planes and curves of his muscles and smiling to herself at the sensation of his curled hair against her fingers. She could picture its color—the rich russet shade that matched Matt's warmth and forcefulness perfectly.

She thought of her gut reaction to that forcefulness, and her conviction that Matt would always be driven to make the kind of career for himself that couldn't possibly fit in with Lily's own plans for her future. Then she shelved those thoughts. For the moment, she was free to enjoy him without worrying about long-term questions. She let her hand wander over the taut skin of his flat stomach and down to the powerful muscles of his thighs, relaxed in sleep. Then her hand slid up, and she found she'd unconsciously aroused him. Matt groaned softly and was pulling Lily toward him as he awakened.

"Trying to seduce me while my guard's down, are you?" he demanded groggily.

Lily grinned at him. "I didn't have to try very hard," she said. There was a playfulness in her smile that Matt had never seen there before.

"True enough," he admitted. "You could seduce me just by looking at me, Lily."

He was fully awake now, and his need for her was just as insistent as though they hadn't made love only a few hours before. Matt picked Lily up in his arms, quilt and all, and strode into the small bedroom. The soft light from a gas streetlight outside filtered through the white gauze curtains, and the brass bed frame shone faintly in the near dark.

He wanted to tell her that ever since the day he'd met her, he'd been thinking of how she would look making love with him. He wanted to explain how challenged he'd felt by her No Trespassing look and how satisfying it was now to see her face without it. She was so lovely, so utterly feminine and desirable.

He didn't tell her any of those things, unless she could read them into his kiss. She'd made it clear that she didn't want to talk about their past or their future, and that was fine with him. There were plenty of other things to do for the present, and Matt was getting on with as many of them as he could.

Their lovemaking this time was anything but rushed, though Lily could feel the same powerful need propelling them. They moved together instinctively, each responsive to

the slightest shift in rhythm or touch. Lily thought fleet-
ingly that time seemed to be playing strange tricks since
she'd stepped into Matt's apartment earlier this evening. She
had no idea now how long it had been since Matt had laid
her down on his bed and she'd felt again the stabbing, satisfying sense of having him inside her. Matt was teaching her
new things with every caress, and she surprised herself at her
own abandon in learning from him. She'd never imagined
a partner so giving, and he made it very easy to give in return.

She seemed to be floating on a restless sea where Matt's
slightest movement gave her pleasure, when she heard him
groan, "Oh, God," and felt his fingers bite into the bare
flesh of her arm. In an instant the warm center of her body
had exploded into new life, and she found herself laughing
and gasping at the same time as they were caught up in the
final wave together.

They managed to crawl under the covers before they fell
asleep this time. The quilt was still strewed over the bed like
a tracing of their entangled bodies. Lily was half-asleep, lost
in the sensation of lying wrapped in Matt's arms, when she
heard him whisper in her ear, "Lily, I love you." She was
too drugged by passion and sleep to register the words as
anything more than just a pleasurable breath of air.

What finally woke her the next morning was a blast from
a car horn in the street outside. She opened her eyes with a
start, sleepily convinced that she'd overslept and the car
horn was summoning her to something important.

It took her a minute to orient herself, and when she did,
her first thought was surprise that Matt was no longer in the
bed beside her. She struggled to a half-sitting position,
leaning on her elbows, and took stock of the situation.

The first thing she noticed was an extraordinary sense of
well-being. She stretched her legs under the covers, and the
faint, remembered sensations of last night came flooding

back. She couldn't have been wrong in her decision to spend the weekend with Matt, when it left her feeling this good!

The next thing that caught her attention was the smell of sausages cooking and coffee brewing. She smiled. Apparently Matt was back to being the perfect host. And a good thing, too, because she seemed to have worked up quite an appetite.

She was halfway out of bed before she realized that she had no clothes with her but her red wool suit, and that was in a state of disarray in the living room. Well, she'd just have to improvise, then. She pulled the quilt around her like a cloak and, barefooted, started toward the kitchen. She could still smell the musky male scent of Matt's body in the folds of the quilt; it was almost like being back in his embrace.

Halfway to the bedroom door, she stopped short. The happy memory of falling asleep in Matt's arms had triggered a more disquieting thought. She'd been more than half-asleep, but she distinctly remembered his murmuring that he loved her.

That's not what I wanted, she thought. All her sense of contentment suddenly vanished. *That's not what I intended at all.* Love implied a commitment and a future, and they'd made a deal that they wouldn't think about those things this weekend. All her misgivings came flooding back more insistent than ever. Surely there were only two choices if she hooked up with another ambitious, demanding lawyer: let herself be swallowed up in his career, or have their separate careers and lives drive them slowly apart.

Besides, the whole magic of this weekend was its island-like remoteness from the problems she dealt with every day. If Matt started insisting they had a future together, that magic would be gone.

She'd better set him straight, and fast. Her mouth was a determined line as she padded across the red Persian carpet in the living room and past the ashy remains of last night's fire in the grate. He'd picked up her clothes and folded them neatly over the back of the sofa, she noted. So he was a good housekeeper, too. But that still didn't mean she was going to sign on for life.

She heard whistling from the direction of the kitchen and realized that Matt was no doubt still in the euphoric state of mind she'd been in herself when she first woke up. It wasn't going to make it easier to be firm with him, but she gathered up all her resolve as she rounded the corner into the small kitchen.

Matt was standing by the stove, wearing a brown heavy dressing gown, busily frying sausages. His face lit up at the sight of her, and he said, "Well, if it isn't the Queen of Sheba."

Lily had forgotten she was wearing nothing but the trailing quilt, and she gathered it a little closer to her body as though she could transform it into a business suit by force of will. Matt's eyes seemed to be hungrily taking in the fact that there was nothing but Lily herself under the quilt, and that was bound to be distracting. She forced herself to sound aloof as she answered.

"If I decide to spend the rest of the weekend here," she said, "I guess I'll have to go out and get something a little more respectable to wear."

Matt laid down his spatula and frowned at her. "*If* you spend the weekend?" he questioned. "I seem to recall you promising you weren't going to run out on me this time."

"That deal had more than one part to it," Lily reminded him. "We weren't going to talk about the future, as I understood it."

"So who's talking about the future?"

"Well, I seem to recall, just before we went to sleep last night, that you said something about loving me." Her voice cracked a little over the words; the look in Matt's eyes was unsettling her.

"I did," he said slowly, watching her face. "And what's wrong with that?"

They were both standing stock-still. Lily wanted more than anything to be back in Matt's embrace, and something in his face suggested that he wanted the same thing, but this had to be said first.

"Love implies some sort of permanent commitment," she said, trying to hold firm. "And that implies a future together. And I'm still very unsure that that would be a good thing. I have the feeling you're trying to rush things, Matt, and I just don't want to be rushed."

Matt looked thoughtfully at the sausages he was cooking. "All right," he said, "I'll buy that. You don't want to be pushed into committing yourself. But Lily, you must know by now that I'm as committed to you as I've ever been to anything."

"Matt—"

"Every day I'm more certain that you and I would be right together. I can't hide that, and after last night, even if I hadn't said I loved you, surely you must know it's true!"

Matt was disturbed at how quickly the serious, studied expression came back to her face. "I don't want a commitment from you," she said. "Not yet, maybe not ever. I don't want to build something up and have it fall apart on me again. I have to know that this can last, before we start talking about love."

Matt sighed. He knew they'd made progress, but at the moment it felt as though they were starting all over again. "And to do that, you have to see me in my new situation, right?"

"That's right."

"For long enough to trust that I mean what I say about not devoting my whole life to the law anymore."

"Right again. Please believe me, Matt. Parts of me would love to say yes to you. Certain parts of me—" she couldn't repress a smile "—already have said yes. But there are still important things for us to clear up."

He knew there were, and he knew from the look in Lily's eyes how important they were to her. He could wait and show her that he was right in their being made for each other. His overwhelming impulse was to seize Lily, carry her back into the bedroom and make love to her until she finally admitted that fact. But he knew she was also right, and he would have to give her more time to learn she could trust him completely with her heart.

Well, if she wanted to be stubborn, he could be stubborn, too. After all, he held records for persistence, Matt reminded himself with a jagged smile. He'd wait her out, however long it took.

Lily couldn't understand the sudden, secretive smile on his face, and it worried her. She'd hoped to be the cool, controlled one in this conversation, but something in Matt's face made her feel as though he'd just taken one jump ahead of her again.

"Well?" she demanded. "Do we have a deal, or not?"

"Deal," he said briefly. "No talk about love, no talk about the law. But I can do whatever else I want, can't I?"

Lily was relieved to let the subject drop and amazed at how quickly her whole body responded to the look of suggestion in Matt's eyes. He was gazing at her as if he could see through the quilt, and her skin tingled as though he'd already touched her.

"Whatever else you want," she echoed, sounding a little breathless. Then she unfolded her crossed arms and invited Matt to step inside.

Nine

Lily was glad she had broached the touchy subject of love and commitment on Saturday morning. Once they'd made their deal to avoid the subject after that, the rest of the weekend was more idyllic than anything Lily had imagined. Without the problem of their future to bother them, or their differences of opinion about their trial in particular and the law in general, she and Matt got along like two old friends. And the ever-new pleasure of their lovemaking took them far beyond the realm of mere friendship.

Once or twice Lily had been bothered by that. What if things *didn't* work out between her and Matt? Memories of this weekend could come back to haunt her and turn all the pleasure she was feeling now into pain. On Saturday night, lying half-awake and listening to Matt's regular breathing beside her as he slept, she had to admit how much he meant to her already. She'd come too far to end things easily, but she still didn't have the evidence she needed to give Matt her fullest trust. It almost made her want to run away again.

With an effort she'd managed to quell those thoughts. The time she was spending with Matt was too enjoyable to waste, and she gave herself up to the luxury of sleeping late, reading the Sunday papers in bed, sending out for Chinese food at outrageously late hours—and finding out over and over again that their powerful physical attraction for each other was the key to creating magic.

Magic came back to earth with a resounding thump first thing on Monday morning. Matt had reluctantly set the alarm before falling asleep, but when he opened his eyes to the sound of persistent beeping, he found that Lily was already out of bed.

"Lily?" he asked sleepily. The bed next to him was no longer warm; she must have been up for quite a while.

"I'm out here," said a faint voice from the living room. Matt groaned to himself. He knew that tone of voice and the expression that went with it. He rolled out of bed and into his dressing gown.

Lily was sitting at the dining room table, already dressed in her red suit. Matt couldn't help staring. How could she look so much the same and yet so completely different? he wondered. She was just as lovely as ever, but all the welcoming signs were gone from her eyes. Just by looking at her, he could feel her holding him at arm's length.

"Couldn't wait to get back to work, I see," he commented, nodding at the file folders Lily had spread out on the table. "And you were accusing me of being married to my job."

"This isn't a job," she replied. She spoke calmly enough, but Matt could tell his words had shaken her slightly. After all, she'd always said that Matt put his career before romance—before anything. Yet here she was already hard at work while Matt had other very definite ideas on his mind.

He decided to press the point. He walked behind her chair and bent down, wrapping her tightly in his arms. When he spoke again, his lips were touching her hair. "What would it take to lure you away from these file folders?'' he whispered, feeling the immediate tremor that ran through her slender body. His own body was answering it urgently.

Lily closed her eyes, knowing it was useless for her to fight against the physical bond between them. She turned her face to the rough surface of Matt's dressing gown and ran her hands over his forearms. Even with her eyes closed she could picture the coppery highlights of the hair that covered the taut muscles under her fingers.

When she spoke, she knew she didn't sound very convincing. ''We have to have our defense ready by ten o'clock,'' she pointed out. ''And we never decided what to do with it on Friday.''

It was a perfectly reasonable answer. Then why did she have to force the words out through lips that could already taste Matt's rough, sweet kisses? She pressed her face more tightly against him and heard the rhythm of his heart very close to her.

''You're right, I suppose.'' His voice held mixed regret and amusement, and she knew he was pleased with the proof of just how strong their attraction for each other was. *This is all wrong,* she almost blurted out. *It's supposed to be me who's making a case for romance, while you're all tied up in work.*

''I'll get right down to business after I've had two things,'' he was continuing. ''A kiss, and a cup of coffee.''

''Which one do you need first?'' she couldn't resist asking.

The answer was swift and decisive. Matt turned her face up to meet his and kissed her with a familiarity and a thoroughness that made her senses reel. He seemed to probe her entire body and make it hum with pure pleasure.

''Which do you think?'' he replied finally, and moved into the kitchen for his coffee without waiting for an answer.

By the time he came back, Lily almost had her professional outer shell back in place. ''Well?'' she said, not giving him time to distract her again. "Have you had any new thoughts about our defense?"

Matt frowned, trying to shift gears from lover to lawyer. "I still don't think we need to change anything," he said. "I think our original strategy is best."

"I don't." Lily sounded firm. "The more I think about it, Matt, the more I'm convinced Tommy's going to win just by sitting there, doing nothing and looking pathetic. We need to fight fire with fire on this one."

Matt sipped the coffee Lily had made and listened to her outline her own plans for the way their defense ought to go. She wanted to scrap the painstaking building up of facts that Matt had started, and stake everything on a simple and personal appeal.

"I think I can do it," she told him. "I know I don't have any courtroom experience, but once I set out to convince someone of something, I'm pretty good at it."

"Even yourself," he couldn't help saying.

"What do you mean?"

"You seem to have convinced yourself that nothing much happened between us this weekend, and now it's just business as usual."

Lily's blue eyes looked troubled, almost angry, he thought. "That was only for this weekend, Matt," she told him. "I couldn't have made it any clearer than that."

"And now what? Do we just pretend it didn't happen?"

"No, of course not, but we—" She made one hand into a fist and let it fall onto the oak table between them. "We have work to do, Matt, and I really think . . ."

She let her words trail off, clearly aware of how strange it was for her to be insisting they work, when Matt wanted to talk about love.

Matt nodded slowly and decided that now wasn't the time to push her too far. She seemed confused by her own feelings for him, and maybe he should just give her time to sort them out. He was supremely confident that they were right for each other, but then he hadn't had Lily's experiences to cloud his judgment.

"All right, then, let's work," he said. Lily looked relieved at his change of pace. "I still don't like your idea. It means putting all our eggs in one basket."

Lily leaned forward, her elbows on the table. "Matt, I'm convinced we won't win if we don't change our strategy. What else have you got to offer?"

Matt looked closely at her. She was very much the professional lawyer at the moment, and he had to admit that her intensity was very hard to resist. Her blue eyes were open and appealing, and she radiated a kind of sincerity that might well counter Tommy Thompson's victim act.

"If we gamble and lose, you realize how much it will end up costing us?" he asked her.

Lily made a face. She'd already calculated what the financial damage might be if Tommy won the case. Matt's share would be covered by his automobile insurance, but Lily's would come straight out of her pocket.

"I realize it," she said. "But Matt, I just have an instinctive feeling that we're going about this the wrong way." She paused and then added, "That's probably just because I'm so idealistic and inexperienced."

Matt winced. He remembered how pushy he'd been about his idea of going into partnership together, and how confidently he'd told her he could shape her future for her. He'd acted as though he had all the answers to her questions, and he knew now that it had been a big mistake. Lily was more than capable of finding her own answers.

He couldn't undo his past mistake, but maybe he could avoid making it again. "If you really feel strongly about it, then I suspect there's something in your idea," he said, and saw her eyes widen in surprise. That pained him; had he really been so negative about her lack of experience? He realized he probably had. "We'll try it your way. Just be warned, though, I've never been happy about losing."

"Join the club." Lily looked serious and pleased at the same time. She'd just been given a challenge, and Matt liked her way of meeting it.

"Go get showered and changed, Malone, or we're going to be late. I'll have breakfast on the table by the time you're done."

Matt followed her orders without protest and did it in record time. "I thought I was supposed to be playing the perfect host," he said ten minutes later around a mouthful of scrambled eggs.

"I'm just paying back hospitality," she replied. Matt felt suddenly as though he might choke. He hadn't meant this weekend as something that needed to be paid back. It was a gift to both of them. And now she was making it clear that she didn't want to be in his debt for anything, from a cup of coffee to a weekend of magic. The case coming up was an important one for both of them, but he'd never had a harder time concentrating on the law than he was having this morning.

By the time they reached the courtroom, both of them were ready to get down to work. Matt dealt quickly with their two remaining witnesses and announced that Lily would be handling their defense from there on.

Lily had learned a lot on Friday from watching Matt, and she was careful to make eye contact with as many people as she could when she spoke. But where Matt was forceful, Lily was gently persuasive, and even in the first few seconds of her speech she could tell that Matt was impressed by the difference.

"Mr. Malone and I have done a lot of work on this case," she began. "But it occurred to us this weekend—" she hoped Matt wouldn't mind being included in "us" even though he'd opposed her plan "—that because we're both lawyers, maybe we've been looking at things too much as lawyers. If we didn't have any legal expertise at all, we would have approached things very differently. For example, I

think we would have made it clear right at the beginning
how sorry we were about Miss Thompson's accident and
how concerned we were about her afterward. Mr. Malone
had to get to Vermont just after it happened, but then he
drove all the way back to Boston to see her at the hospital.
He found me already there, as a matter of fact. You may
think I was simply delaying driving through rush-hour
traffic all the way to Hartford, but I really was concerned.''

Lily smiled, and the elusive dimple in her left cheek made
an appearance. Matt sat back in his chair, watching with
growing admiration. Lily had been right. She might be inexperienced in a courtroom, but she did understand something of human nature, and the faces of the jury were
interested and receptive.

"We even left her some flowers," she added as if it were
an afterthought. "I don't know if she realized that."

She half turned in Tommy's direction and was rewarded
by the first real show of personality that Tommy had given
the court. "Of course I did," the old woman said in spite of
her lawyer's warning hand on her wrist. "Red roses, the
nurse said. A whole dozen. The last fellow that hit me never
even sent a card. Some people can be stingy, I can tell you.''

She seemed ready to tell the court more, but her lawyer
whispered something in her ear and she subsided. But Lily
was satisfied. At last the jury had some notion that Tommy
was not just the frail victim she'd appeared to be on Friday.

"Anyway," Lily went on, "what we wanted to do today
was just give you our side of what happened. I understand
Miss Thompson's point of view. It must be terrifying to try
to negotiate Boston traffic when you can't see—''

Once again, Tommy couldn't keep quiet. "I've never been
terrified in my life," she piped up. "It's only when people
start turning me all around and putting their hands on me.
I can't stand to be touched by strangers, never could." Once
again her lawyer managed to quiet her, but once again Lily
had succeeded in getting Tommy to show her true colors.
And she could see the jury members digesting this infor-

mation and wondering, as Lily had wondered, how you could quickly direct a blind person without touching them.

"I understand that now," she said, "but at the time I was just concerned with helping Miss Thompson safely across the street."

The judge admonished Tommy not to talk out of turn and asked Lily to proceed.

She did, telling the story from her point of view and Matt's, with a simple clearness that left no doubt she was telling the truth. While in law school, Lily had learned to use her voice to its best advantage, and she was doing that now, making it caress and convince where shouting would have done no good at all.

When Tommy took the witness stand, the contrast between Lily's smooth, reasonable questions and the blind woman's peppery answers was glaring. It became obvious to everyone that Tommy would fight simply for the sake of fighting and that Lily and Matt were just the convenient excuse for this particular fight. As the morning drew to a close, Tommy had shifted from victim to aggressor, and Lily could see Matt almost grinning outright with satisfaction.

It took the jury ten minutes to decide in favor of Lily and Matt, and the judge had some extra comments to add. "I must say I'm obliged to Ms. Martineau for putting things into perspective for us," he said. "And I'd like to add that should Miss Thompson feel moved to bring any similar suits in the future—" he looked at Tommy with an expression that suggested he thought her quite capable of doing that "—she should consider that there are cases where no one is at fault, and that pointing fingers of blame in those cases is simply not appropriate."

The noon recess was announced, and the usual hush of the courtroom changed to the hum of conversation. Lily made her way back to where Matt was standing, trying to subdue the grin that wanted to break out on her face. By the time she reached him, the grin had won.

"Tell me, Mr. Malone," she said, her eyes shining, "do experienced lawyers jump up and down after winning cases?"

"It's considered unprofessional," he told her, putting an arm around her shoulder and grinning back, "but in this case I'd say you deserve to do it. Congratulations, Lily. It's a good feeling, isn't it?"

"It sure is," Lily acknowledged. She leaned against Matt's side, enjoying his strength and nearness. "For almost four months I've been sitting in my little office in that insurance building, wondering why I decided to be a lawyer. A couple of times I've been on the verge of giving up, but not anymore. I know I can be good at this."

"You're right." Matt's face grew a little more serious. "Most people start out with low-key cases and someone to lead them by the hand. You really jumped in with both feet, and you did a hell of a job with it."

Matt's compliments went straight to Lily's head. She might have serious reservations about getting romantically involved with a lawyer, but praise from a very highly regarded one like Matt was more than welcome.

"I'll tell you what," she said buoyantly. "When I called Sarah on Saturday, I asked her to tell the people at work that I wouldn't be in at all today. So I'm in no rush to get back to Hartford. What do you say to a celebration lunch?"

Matt hooked his arm through hers as they left the courtroom. "Sounds good to me. Why don't we go down by the harbor and—" He stopped suddenly, then swore. "We won't have time to go far," he said apologetically. "I forgot I have a court appearance at two."

He didn't like what he was seeing in her face. Surely not, those light-blue eyes were saying to him. Don't do this again.

He hurried to explain. "Remember I told you I was wrapping up my last case for Sloan and Baker today?" he asked, tightening his grip on her arm as he felt her muscles tense. "This is it—a judge's ruling on an appeal. One more consultation with a Sloan and Baker client, and it's all over.

That makes two things to celebrate. Lily, you can't think of running out on me now.''

She hadn't said anything about running out, but the look in her eyes scared him. He had to convince her to stay. This was the beginning of all the things he was passionately hoping they could share.

"Are you *sure* this is really your last Sloan and Baker case?" she asked him, her voice low. "You were so sure you'd be all done before the New Year, remember. What if something else comes up?"

"I'll turn it down."

She didn't reply to that, but he could read her thoughts. So far he'd always put his work first; he had to admit she had that point. He couldn't think of a completely convincing answer to her unspoken challenge so he fell back on what had held them together up till now, in spite of everything—the spark of sensuality that always broke into an open flame at their first touch.

"I'll turn it down, I promise," he said quietly, turning so that his mouth was close to hers. He didn't move to kiss her, but the tug of attraction was so strong that he almost didn't need to. He could feel her quivering inside and somehow knew that she was feeling uncertainty mixed with desire.

"Let's go and have lunch," he urged, "and then you can come and watch the last gasp of the old Matt Malone."

She nodded without speaking, and Matt's heart constricted into an anxious fist inside him. For all the loving they'd shared this weekend, he knew Lily was far from won. She could bolt away again at any moment. He could see it in those light blue eyes.

"Lily," he said, and his voice was as gentle and persuasive as he knew how to make it sound. "I have something to confess. When I told you to go ahead and follow your instincts on our case, I was going against my own professional judgment. I hoped you were right, but my experience told me you might not be."

"Then why did you give in?"

"Because you felt so strongly about it, and because I didn't want you to think I was trying to dictate your every move."

"Thanks," she said, "but I don't understand—"

"I know it sounds as if I'm changing the subject, but I'm not. What I'm trying to say is I think it's your turn to stop listening to what your experience tells you. Yes, I'm cutting lunch short for a courtroom appearance, and yes, I did say I'd be cut loose from Sloan and Baker by now, and yes, I've done this to you in the past. But every instinct I've got tells me that this will be the last time it happens this way. Do you understand that?"

"You're trying to tell me I should trust your instincts, the way you trusted mine," Lily said slowly.

"That's it." The courtroom was sufficiently empty now for Matt to draw her even closer and kiss the sweet-smelling skin behind her ear. That spot, he'd discovered to his satisfaction this past weekend, could be counted on to turn Lily's breathing into a throaty murmur. Matt loved the way her skin felt to his lips, and the things it did to him inside whenever he kissed her.

He could feel her heartbeat picking up speed as he held her against his side. "Say you won't run away, Lily," he whispered into her thick hair. "I couldn't stand it if you left now."

Lily sighed. Her feelings were in enough confusion without Matt's sensual embrace to stir things up even further. But she decided to stay with her first impulse—lunch to celebrate their courtroom victory—and hope that things would sort themselves out somehow.

It was two o'clock when Lily settled herself back in a courtroom for the second time that day, this time as a spectator rather than a participant. The opportunity to watch Matt at work was a tempting one. Perhaps by seeing him in his Sloan and Baker guise, she would be able to fill in some of the gaps that still worried her.

Her first impression, as always, was what a good-looking man he was. He'd chosen to put on a charcoal-gray suit that morning, and even in the dark color he was eye-catching. It was far more than the dull glow of his red silk tie or the gleam of his gold tiepin. His forceful personality came leaping out and made him a natural center of attention.

Lily remembered the comment he'd made when they were both dressed and ready to leave for the courtroom that morning. "Quite a pair of bookends, aren't we?" he'd said, looking at their reflection in the big gold-framed mirror in his hallway. And they had been. Lily's jewel-red suit and Matt's distinguished dark one had complemented each other perfectly, especially when Matt had drawn her into his arms and their two figures had merged into one.

Lily frowned as she watched Matt from the back row of the courtroom. She'd been trying so hard to keep her distance from him this morning, but with every touch he had undermined her resolve. It had worried her then, as she was worrying now. Was she already too close to Matt Malone to back out if she wanted to?

She made herself concentrate on what was happening in front of her, although her eyes kept straying toward Matt's attractive, muscular figure. The case seemed to involve a ruling on whether Matt's client had a right to an appeal or not. At first Matt argued in the same tone of voice she'd heard him use on Friday, almost as though he was having a conversation with the judge.

But when the decision seemed likely to go against him, he changed his tactics. His voice became more forceful, and he spoke as though the judge's decision would affect Matt's personal life. Not bad, Lily thought. You'd almost think he'd be doing this even if he wasn't being paid.

Clearly Matt had done his homework—she remembered the long hours he said he put in when working on an important case—and he seemed well armed with reasons why his client should be entitled to an appeal. But beyond that, Lily could tell that his manner was influencing the judge, and the realization gave her a chill. After all, this was what Matt was so good at—arguing until he got what he wanted, in whatever tone of voice would get results.

She closed her eyes, remembering how single-mindedly he'd been pursuing her since last October. She remembered, too, how much he hated to lose at anything. What if she was nothing more than a prize to be won like an important court case? She'd challenged him the way the law did. And he'd used the same technique to win her over—first cajoling, then demanding, never giving up.

She could see the judge was about to come down on Matt's side. But that didn't mean Lily Martineau was so easily persuaded. She'd had the right idea that morning, after all, when she'd tried to keep her distance from Matt's considerable charms. And she'd keep that distance until he'd proved once and for all that his hard-driven, workaholic days were over and done with.

She stood up as the judge announced his decision, intending to make a quick getaway. But in the scene of handshaking and congratulations that followed around Matt and his client, Matt happened to glance up, and Lily knew he'd caught her movement. That was what she got for wearing red, she thought.

She didn't want to stay and talk to Matt. She had a lot to think about, and she needed to think in peace. Peace and Matt were two things seldom found in the same room together, she knew by now. But as she was making her way to the door, she heard him call her name.

"Lily, wait! Just another minute or two, and I'll be done here."

Against her better judgment, she waited. But two minutes is all you get, she told him mentally. She'd spent too many hours of her life waiting while Alexander finished up last-minute business, and it was something she had never liked. It was hard to be the outsider, waiting in a courtroom full of people she didn't know.

That feeling went way back, she knew. It had dogged her all through her ten years with her aunt and uncle. She'd never fit into her adopted family, not because she'd been unwelcome, but simply because she and her relatives had had nothing in common. She certainly wasn't going to stand around feeling like a fifth wheel for any longer than she had to.

"Sure we can't tempt you into staying to take care of the appeal for us, Matt?" one of the three-piece-suited men was saying.

Matt smiled. "Sorry, Clay," he said. "Believe it or not, I intended to be all done at Sloan and Baker ages ago, but Derek talked me into seeing you through this."

"Didn't have to talk very much, as I recall," said another man. Lily scanned his long, craggy features and slightly rumpled gray suit and realized that this must be Derek Sloan, the managing partner of the firm and Matt's mentor. "Matt's always taken a personal interest in your company's fortunes, haven't you, Matt?"

If Matt was less enthusiastic than his boss, Lily couldn't tell. He seemed so utterly at home in this gathering of businessmen. Could he ever really settle down to the kind of practice he was proposing in Brattleboro?

She doubted it more than ever. His two minutes were up, she noted, and once more she started for the courtroom door.

Once more he caught her. This time he moved up the aisle and took her arm. "Sorry," he said with an uncomfortable smile, "but you know how last-minute business drags on. I won't be long. Come and be introduced."

Matt's strong grip propelled her down the aisle and into the circle of men. She shook hands all around, and then they went back to their discussion.

"I'd value your recommendation for an attorney to take care of the appeal," the man named Clay was saying.

"Anyone Derek recommends..."

"...feel more comfortable if you'd change your mind, Matt..."

"It all depends on which judge you end up with..."

"McNamara eats out of Matt's hand, always has..."

Lily felt a tug of impatience in her stomach. In spite of his words, Matt was making no move to leave. She looked at the faces of the men around her and remembered what Matt had told her about the case they were involved in. It had to do with one firm taking over another, with no personal issues at stake, just corporate profits. And somehow the serious faces around her seemed to mirror that.

Including Matt's. She'd been very close to falling in love with the man she'd spent last weekend with, but this was a very different man. It hurt to know just how different he could become, but she was still glad she'd found out. Instinct and experience had told her Matt wasn't right for her, and instinct and experience had turned out to be right.

"I've really got to go, Matt," she said in a low voice, and detached herself from the group before he had time to protest. But her quick getaway was hampered by the fact that Matt followed on her heels after a quick "Excuse me, gentlemen," to the men around him.

Just outside the courtroom door he caught her and blocked her way. She stared levelly at the broad expanse of his chest, refusing to meet his eyes. "You seem to be in the way," she said, trying unsuccessfully to step around him.

"You bet I am," he replied hotly, "and I intend to stay there until you tell me what you think you're doing."

"I'm leaving," she said bluntly. "I had some questions about you that still weren't answered, Matt, but I think I've got the answers now."

"What kind of questions?" His hands were on his hips, and his voice was threateningly close to anger.

"Questions like 'Will you really be satisfied drawing up wills after managing corporate takeovers?' I don't think you will be."

"I thought we'd gotten beyond making snap assumptions about each other."

"It's not a snap assumption." Still she didn't look directly at him. "I watched you closely in that courtroom, Matt, and I think you're more a part of that kind of legal world than you realize."

"Maybe I'm just a good actor, did you ever think of that?"

"Oh, yes," she said bitterly. "I've thought of that. And it's one of those things that scares me about you."

"*Scares* you?" The naked surprise in Matt's voice made her look up suddenly.

"Yes, scares me." Her voice trembled no matter how she tried to keep it steady. "You know why I've had serious doubts about this all along. And the more I see of you, the more convinced I am that our relationship will end up hurting both of us, if we go any further with it."

"Lily, you're just burying yourself with what happened in the past." There it was, that caressing, persuading tone of voice. Twenty minutes ago, he'd used it to persuade a judge to let one corporation take over another. Now he was using it on her. "If you never let yourself take a chance, you're never going to find a relationship that means anything."

He ran a hand along her arm, encouraging her to trust him, but she moved away. "Yes, I will," she said stubbornly. "I know I will, someday. But it has to be with someone who wants the same things out of life that I do. A career, yes, but also a home life, and a family."

Her voice was faltering in a serious way by now. Until she'd said the words out loud, she hadn't realized just how much she'd come to hope that Matt Malone might turn out to be different than he seemed. She'd already done what she'd promised herself not to do—come too far to turn back without pain. And that thought threatened to make the catch in her voice turn to tears.

Matt took hold of her, and his voice was low and urgent. "I can be that person, Lily," he said, shaking her slightly as though he could force her to believe it. "Just don't give up on us now."

"There is no 'us!'" she shot back. Once more she stepped away from the embrace she would have loved to throw herself into. "There's no point to going on, Matt. Once you've been in practice in Vermont for a year, maybe you can give me a call. Unless you find you're working just as many hours there as you are here."

Matt gritted his teeth. "Is that what it'll take to convince you?" he demanded.

"Yes."

"Lily, how can I make it through a year without you?"

She didn't want to hear his arguments. Their weekend of passion and companionship was going to be hard enough to forget as it was. "Somehow I think you'll survive, Matt," she said. "Anyone who loves a fight as much as you do is bound to come out on top."

So far she'd managed to subdue the tears that were stinging her eyes, but the look of utter frustration on Matt's face was wearing her down. If she gave way to the tears, how would she ever resist the temptation to put her hands on Matt's strong shoulder and take comfort in his arms? And that would be the end of all her good intentions.

Better to leave now with some dignity. Just as she'd done last November, she thought, only now the wrench was so much more painful. "Goodbye, Matt," she said with finality, and turned away from him down the long corridor. She almost expected him to follow, but for once he didn't live up to his reputation as a fighter. This time, he let her go.

Ten

"I knew I did the right thing in talking you into buying a new dress," Sarah said triumphantly as Lily emerged from her bedroom the next Saturday.

"Part of me agrees with you," Lily said, smoothing the skirt that fit her slender hips to perfection, "and part of me keeps pointing out that just before I'm going to be unemployed is not the time to be splurging on new clothes!"

"I can refute that, Your Honor. In the first place, Ms. Martineau has barely spent a nickel on new clothes in four months. In the second place, if a woman can't buy a new outfit for her very first art opening, I'd like to know when she can. And in the third place, that dress looks absolutely stunning on you. It'll be a wonder if anybody looks at your paintings after they catch a glimpse of you."

Lily laughed for what felt like the first time all week. "All right, you talked me into it again," she said. The dress Sarah was so enthusiastic about was a dusky twilight blue, with full, draped sleeves and a close-fitting waistline and skirt.

Something in its shade made Lily's eyes come alive. She'd accented the dress with a silver necklace and earrings, and the January day was dry enough today that she was risking delicate blue leather shoes instead of boots, and a new pair of nylons with a faint blue sheen to them.

She still hadn't gotten over the surprise that had prompted her to buy the dress. She'd arrived home from Boston on Monday evening feeling confused and bereft, only to find that all her new watercolors, the ones she'd done of the Vermont mountains, had disappeared from the walls of the apartment.

"Sarah, where are my paintings?" she'd asked, too numb to be worried. It had taken a while to get the truth from Sarah. Certain that the paintings were good enough to be a part of the upcoming art show at the public library, Sarah had taken photographs of them several weeks ago and submitted them to the judges. The paintings had won a prize and were included in the exhibit, which was opening that weekend.

"The judges said they were some of the best amateur work they've had submitted in years," Sarah had added, still not sure whether Lily was pleased or angry.

Lily hadn't been quite sure herself. She was so buffeted by her conflicting feelings about Matt that the added surprise of the art show had barely sunk in. But now, by the end of the week, she was positively excited about it. And a good thing, too, she'd told herself more than once. With the opening to look forward to, she hadn't spent quite *all* her time thinking of Matt.

She'd given Sarah a condensed version of what had happened in the courtroom on Monday, and Sarah had been tactful about not bringing up the subject again. Now, as Lily finished dressing on Saturday, her roommate seemed more concerned with Lily's impending unemployment.

"You know, that job in the legal department is still open," she said. "I know the company's pleased with what you've done on your survey; all you have to do is say the word, and I'll talk to them about hiring you full-time.''

"I appreciate the offer," Lily said, "but I have a strong feeling I shouldn't take a job that doesn't really appeal to me.''

A strong feeling aided and abetted by Matt's advice on the subject. No matter what Lily was thinking about, she always seemed to come up against Matt Malone.

In thought only. Against all her expectations, he hadn't called since their meeting last Monday. And that surprised her, knowing what she did of Matt's character. Up until this week, he'd been almost maddeningly persistent. And now he seemed to have forgotten all about her.

Had she somehow managed to convince him just how sure she was that their romance couldn't work? Lily had puzzled over it until her head ached. Nothing about it seemed to make sense. He'd been in the throes of moving, she reminded herself. Setting up his new home and business was no doubt taking up all his time.

But that didn't fit with his passionate claims about how much she meant to him. If she'd been all that important in his life, wouldn't he have found five minutes to pick up a telephone and call?

Every time that thought struck her, she had to remind herself that she'd told him over and over she didn't want to get further involved with him, and she should be grateful that for whatever reason, he was leaving her alone. She *was* grateful, she insisted to herself. It was just that she was also puzzled—and very lonely.

She had even remarked on it to Sarah, saying one evening how odd it seemed not to have Matt leaving messages all the time.

"It is a little odd," Sarah had agreed. There had been something in her roommate's manner that had struck Lily as odd in itself.

"You don't sound quite convinced," Lily had commented. "Or has he called, after all?"

"No, not when I was here, anyway," Sarah had replied. She'd seemed distracted, and Lily had put it down to the fact that their kitchen table was covered with documents, and Sarah was neck-deep in legal homework.

By Saturday Lily had managed to turn her mind to thoughts of seeing her paintings displayed in public for the first time. All her life she'd been painting to satisfy herself, but this was different.

"My first court case and my first art exhibit, all in one week," she said to Sarah as they left the apartment together. "Life may seem a little dull for a while after this." She laughed.

And then her laughter faded at the thought that life already seemed a little duller without Matt in it. She'd lost track of the number of times she'd relived their weekend together, aching for the touch of his lips and the heady passion of their lovemaking. No matter how often she told herself that she'd done the right thing, she couldn't seem to banish the longing she felt.

The exhibit had already opened when they arrived at the library. The curator, a tall, distinguished older woman, introduced herself and was delighted to finally meet Lily.

"Our reluctant artist!" she exclaimed with a smile. "I'm so glad you're here. Come over and meet the judges, my dear; they're all going to tell you that you've been much, much too modest about your talent."

Sarah winked at Lily as she was swept off in a round of introductions. Quite a lot of people seemed to have heard about Sarah's ruse in entering Lily's work in the exhibit, and as the curator had warned her, she was told over and over again that she should show her paintings more often.

It was a while before she could get away by herself to look at the watercolors. She'd always been satisfied by her paintings, and over the years she'd given several as gifts to friends who'd admired them. But it was a new experience to look at her work and realize that complete strangers enjoyed it, too. She stood in front of one picture for some time, a large picture of a stormy sky over darkened mountains, and wondered what it was about this particular set of pictures that was disturbing her. And then a voice behind her gave her the answer.

"They look angry."

Lily realized two things simultaneously. The first was that the voice was right—the pictures were angry and much more riveting than any of her other work.

The second thing was that the voice belonged to Matt Malone. She whirled around, too glad to see him even to wonder how he'd managed to find her.

"They also look familiar," Matt was saying, sounding as detached as any casual visitor to the exhibit might have been. "I could swear those views were lifted straight off my property in Vermont."

"Borrowed, maybe, not lifted," Lily corrected him. "And you're right about them looking angry. I guess I was angrier than I realized when I painted them."

Neither of them was looking at the paintings. Lily was thinking that Matt seemed tired, and it wasn't just that he had slight dark circles under his eyes. The forcefulness she'd always found both intriguing and a little bit threatening wasn't in evidence today. He was lacking some of his usual sparkle, but there was an intensity in his dark brown eyes that more than made up for it.

"Are you angry now?" he asked her softly. He raised his hand and gently caressed the side of her face. As it always did, his touch drew her closer to him, and the warmth of his fingers brought a faint dusky flush to her cheeks. "I realize I've dropped in without warning."

"No, I'm not angry." She wondered if her eyes were telling him what she was really feeling—that the moment she admitted to herself how much she loved his touch and his quiet, seductive voice, she had to admit as well that she loved *him*. All of him, from his muscular frame to the quirky grin, which always seemed to lurk in the curve of his mouth. She didn't know where to go next with Matt Malone, but the instant he ran his hand over her skin, she knew she didn't want to go on without him.

"I'm just a little curious, that's all," she went on. Her eyes were locked with his, part of the almost tangible current of feeling between them. "How did you know where to find me? Or is it just part of your new routine to spend your Saturdays checking out art exhibits?"

He grinned. "Who knows? I'm enjoying this one. And it sure beats working all weekend. Maybe I'll make this a permanent feature of the new, improved Matt Malone."

She couldn't keep the smile from her face. It felt so good to see him again. "Sounds like a good idea," she told him. "So how does it feel to be new and improved?"

He frowned slightly. "I haven't had time to think about that yet," he said. "I've been thinking too hard about you." With one sure movement he captured her hand and planted a kiss in the center of her palm, which made her blood sing in her ears. "God, Lily, every time I see you I think to myself, 'That's the loveliest she's ever looked,' and then the next time you manage to look even lovelier. You're going to drive me crazy if you keep this up."

"And you're going to drive *me* crazy if you kiss me like that again," she whispered throatily. She knew he wouldn't have been Matt Malone if he'd resisted a challenge like that, and as he kissed the soft flesh of her upraised palm again, her breathing betrayed her with a sigh of pure passion.

"Don't look now, but there's a bevy of art lovers heading our way," she murmured. "Maybe we should be a little more sedate." She knew both their faces were flushed with something far beyond artistic appreciation.

"Or maybe we should go somewhere where we don't *have* to be sedate," he responded.

Lily looked around the room. She'd done her official duty in meeting the judges and chatting with the curator and the head librarian. Her whole body was in a turmoil at being this close to Matt again, and she knew it was only a matter of time before their potent attraction got the better of them.

She'd missed him so achingly this past week that she couldn't possibly deny herself the comfort of being nestled in his arms again. Maybe, in that case, a quick escape was in order.

"All right," she said, and saw his smile widen with satisfaction. "Let me just tell my roommate that I'm leaving."

"Give her my regards," Matt said, and smiled even more at her puzzled look.

"I smell a conspiracy," she said, "which you can explain to me later."

She found Sarah engaged in a conversation with one of the other artists. "Excuse me," Lily said, "but I just wanted to let you know I'm, well, leaving a bit early."

Sarah smiled. There was a faint echo of Matt's satisfaction in her expression. "Found a friend, did you?" she asked innocently.

"Actually, he found me, as I expect you already know." Lily grinned back, and the other artist looked puzzled. "Thanks again for getting me into this show in spite of myself, Sarah. If I'm ever looking for an agent, I'll let you know."

Sarah groaned. "Sure," she said. "I'll do it in my spare time. Have fun, Lily."

Sarah, like most lawyers, spent a hefty percentage of her time on her work, and Lily knew that a week ago she would have used that as ammunition against Matt. But something inside her seemed to have suddenly switched sides, and for the first time she found herself feeling more confident about Matt's promises to change his life-style.

When she rejoined him, he reached out an arm and wrapped her in an embrace that reinforced all those new, unexpected feelings. He drew her into the hallway, away from the roomful of polite art lovers, and Lily abandoned herself to the sensations of his warm, searching mouth against hers and the powerful muscles of his arms holding her close.

"Lily Martineau, don't you ever run out on me again," he muttered. He seemed to be trying to crack a rib or two, but she didn't care. "You're as glad to see me as I am to see you, and don't you dare deny it."

"I—I won't even try, Matt." She raised her face to his again, but this time she was the one who sought out his lips. She could feel him responding eagerly, and she gasped at the strength of her own desire. Wildly she wished that both of them could suddenly be transported somewhere, anywhere, where they could be alone together.

Matt seemed to share her thoughts. "If we don't get out of here soon, I'm going to lose all control and do something that I think librarians frown on even more than overdue books," he said, and Lily smiled in spite of her crazily beating heart.

"I know what you mean," she said. "Where are you parked?"

"At the far end of the library lot," he replied. He kept one arm around her shoulders as they left the building.

"So tell me," she said, skipping down the stairs in unison with him, "how *did* you manage to show up here at just the right time?"

"I enlisted your roommate as an ally," he confessed. "We were practically fast friends already, from all the messages she's taken this winter. I called on Tuesday evening—you were out somewhere—and told her I was in desperate straits because I couldn't see you."

"Desperate, huh?"

"Yes, woman, and don't you grin about it. Anyway, I asked Sarah what she thought would happen if I just showed up suddenly on your doorstep, and she said why didn't I show up suddenly at the art show, instead. She thought you might not appreciate being cornered in your bedroom."

"She was right." Lily was glad of her friend's insight. If Matt had simply pounded on her door with no warning, she might very well have refused to open up. But today, it had somehow been much easier to admit how much she'd wanted to see him.

"So I suspected. And voilà, here I am."

"Voilà yourself." They'd reached Matt's Jeep, which was spattered with a layer of salt and mud and not nearly so gleamingly new as it had been last fall. Matt turned the key in the passenger door lock, and held it open for her.

Before she could make a move to climb inside, she found herself back in the satisfying warmth of his arms. She leaned her head against his broad shoulder, the feel of his breath against her bare neck making her tremble with delight. Somewhat shakily she managed to ask him, "Matt, where are we going?"

He raised his head slowly, and his face was serious as he said, "I thought we might take a run up to Vermont."

"To your house?" Clearly both of them were reliving their last expedition to Brattleboro and how many raw edges that encounter had exposed. Lily asked herself if things had changed enough between them to attempt the trip again.

Then he kissed her again as though he couldn't help himself, and Lily gave herself up to the sweet, surging desire that pulsed through her. *Yes*, her whole body was telling her, *things have changed enough to take another chance*.

"We'll need to stop by my apartment to get some more clothes," she said when she could speak again. "I can't stomp through the woods in Italian leather high heels."

"Does that mean you're saying yes?" he demanded.

"Yes." The single word came out on a sigh that sounded suspiciously like relief.

She'd never been in a vehicle with Matt before, she realized. It was surprising how comfortable it felt to be next to him in the small space. Surprising, in fact, how she felt she belonged there.

He insisted on following her up the staircase when they arrived at her apartment building. "The perfect host never lets a guest carry her own bags," he explained.

"Been reading Miss Manners, have you?"

"No, just fishing for any excuse not to let you out of my sight. Nice mirror," he commented, following her into her bedroom. "Too bad somebody covered it up with all these little yellow messages." He pushed the door closed behind them and added, "You know, it's very muddy up in Vermont just now."

"Is it?"

"*Very* muddy. And even though that dress makes you look like twilight personified, I don't think you'd better risk wearing it in the woods."

"I wasn't planning to." She gave him a demure smile. "But I'm perfectly capable of changing into a pair of blue jeans by myself."

"And deprive me of earning my merit badge in helpfulness? Forget it, lady."

He was reaching both arms behind her back as he spoke, beginning to undo the long row of little buttons that closed the dress.

"Matt . . ." She wanted this desperately and had wanted it for what seemed like a long time. Her faint protest was merely a reflex.

"What?" His voice was blurred with passion.

"If Sarah comes back . . ."

He looked into her eyes, and the wicked grin she found so seductive was gleaming out at her. "Do you really care?" he asked her.

His fingers were expertly dealing with the row of buttons, and beneath her lacy brassiere she could feel the centers of her breasts hardening into taut circles, begging for the touch of Matt's fingers and tongue. He was pushing the blue dress from her shoulders now, exposing the silky expanse of her skin.

"No," she breathed. "I don't really care."

Matt was wearing a heavy dark green sweater over a black turtleneck, and Lily slid her hands under both layers of clothing to touch his warm bare skin. He was so strong, so alive, just the touch of the curly russet hair on his broad chest was enough to bring her to the boiling point.

"I think I've been dreaming about this twenty-four hours a day," he said through clenched teeth. She heard him groan as her hands traveled across the planes and hollows of his upper body. His heartbeat, as her fingers rested above it, felt like a racing engine.

Quickly he stripped off his clothes and turned his attention back to her dress. He made short work of the narrow belt around her waist, and then with a long breath of anticipation he pushed the whole dusky blue mass over her hips and let it fall into a pile on the floor. Lily unhooked her bra and pulled off her slip and panties. She couldn't wait any longer to feel the solid length of him against her body.

As before, the sensation of their unclothed embrace made her cry out with pleasure. He was throbbing against her, clasping her slender body as though he was holding life itself in his hands. Lily let her head fall back, eyes closed, lost in her own need for him as he awakened every inch of her skin with his touch.

Last weekend they had taken time to get to know each other, to explore. Now they knew, and something more primal was driving both of them on. Matt clasped her rounded bottom in his strong hands and whispered against her throat, "Lift up your legs, Lily." His passion-roughened voice was like a song in her ears. "Wrap yourself around me."

She did as he told her, feeling the hard muscles in his calves and thighs as she moved her legs over them. He lifted her, too, until she was twined around him like a vine encircling a mighty oak.

"Please, Matt," she almost sobbed, dizzied by the force of her desire for him. "I've wanted you so much."

"That's what I wanted to hear." His voice was ragged, satisfied.

And with one thrust he buried himself deeply inside her, reaching for and finding the hidden source of all her pleasure. They moved together instinctively, hungrily, and neither one of them was fully aware of the exact moment when Matt moved across the small bedroom and laid Lily down on her bed, still inside her.

The only thought in Lily's mind was that this was right and inevitable, and even that thought vanished as some inner rhythm shifted speeds and urged their movements to quicken, and quicken even more. Each subtle change of position made the anticipation more overwhelming, until they both abandoned themselves entirely and sought out the climax that was maddening them.

It happened so suddenly that for an instant Lily thought she knew what it meant to see stars. Certainly some kind of radiance danced behind her closed eyes for a long, pulsating moment, and she heard her hoarse cry mingled with Matt's as though both sounds came from a long way away. Then slowly the familiar surroundings of her room came back into everyday focus, and the shattering experience she and Matt had just shared subsided into the sweet release of shared pleasure.

Finally Matt spoke. "So," he said lazily, "all ready to go to Vermont?"

She smiled. "Ready when you are," she replied.

She twirled her fingers in the small auburn curls at the base of his neck, and neither of them moved again for a long time.

Eleven

It was dark when they got to Matt's house. The night was too overcast for stars, and as they climbed the stairs to the porch, Lily commented, "I always forget how dark it gets in the country."

"Dark and cold," Matt agreed. "But once I liven up the fire in the wood stove, we should be warm enough."

Inside, the big log house was completely transformed. Carpets covered the floors, and a new sofa and two chairs sat in front of the fireplace. One thing, however, was still the same—Matt's telephone still sat on the stone hearth. And two minutes after they walked in the door, it started to ring.

"Should I answer it?" Lily asked.

Matt was busy loading logs into a big wood stove in the center of the main room. "Don't you dare," he said. "The answering machine is on. They can leave a message if it's important."

That was a step in the right direction, Lily thought. The phone rang again while they ate their dinner at Matt's an-

tique kitchen table, and again he ignored it. And then, late
at night, when they were just falling asleep after an hour of
lovemaking that had been slow, sensuous and filled with an
unimaginable tenderness, Lily heard the phone's shrill
ringing again.

"Go away," Matt muttered. He sounded asleep already,
and Lily smiled as she heard the beep of the answering machine in the next room. This was a far cry from the Matt
Malone who had been so bound up in his job in Boston. *In
some ways,* she added mentally. In other ways he was just
the same, and her smile broadened as she thought about
those other ways. She moved even closer to the warmth of
his body under the quilt, and drifted off to sleep.

There was sunshine flooding the room in the morning,
and Lily made a slight protesting noise as she opened her
eyes. The sound woke Matt, and he pulled her toward him.

"Morning," he said indistinctly.

"It sure is," Lily said. "Did you design your bedroom so
it gets full sunlight at the crack of dawn?"

"It isn't supposed to," Matt said. "What time is it?"

Lily lifted her watch from the night table and found that
it was almost ten. "We've been sleeping in," she announced.

"Good for us." He pulled her a little closer yet. "We deserve it."

It was almost noon by the time they got up, and by that
time they both felt they deserved breakfast. The telephone
was ringing again as they entered the kitchen.

"Do you always get this many calls?" Lily wondered out
loud.

"Probably just wrong numbers," Matt said offhand-
edly. "Or people trying to sell me things I don't want to buy.
Nothing to worry about."

But after breakfast, when Lily had announced her intention of trying out Matt's newly installed shower and headed

for the bathroom, she could hear the shrill ringing again. She couldn't help wondering what the calls were about and if Matt would eventually wonder the same thing and answer the phone.

She found out sooner than she'd expected. She didn't take long in the shower, and while she was brushing her hair in the warm, steamy bathroom, she heard clicks and beeps from the living room that told her Matt was checking the messages on his answering machine. She couldn't hear the words, just a woman's high-pitched, anxious voice.

Lily's heart seemed to contract a little bit. She'd made her decision about Matt by now. No matter what they still had to work out between them, she couldn't imagine being separated from him again. And she was sure they could do it. But she'd hoped her newly made decision wouldn't be tested quite this soon.

"Anything interesting on the machine?" she asked casually when she returned to the living room. Matt was laying a fire in the fireplace, and she couldn't see his face.

"Not really." His voice was brusque and uninformative, without its usual candid ring.

"Did you have plans for today?" Lily was watching him closely.

"Beyond sitting in front of a roaring fire with you, I hadn't planned anything," he said. "Care for more coffee?"

He went to get it before she'd even answered. The phone messages had unsettled him, she could tell. He was avoiding meeting her eyes, something he'd never done before.

He made a valiant effort to ignore whatever was bothering him, she had to admit. He spent part of the afternoon giving her a top-to-bottom tour of his house, and his obvious pride in the home he'd created seemed to take his mind off the phone calls.

"Why such a big house?" Lily wanted to know.

Matt shrugged. "Maybe you're not the only one who's thinking in terms of having a family some day," he said.

She suggested continuing the tour and taking a trip into Brattleboro to see his law office. But as he showed her around the renovated two-story house he'd bought for his business, he seemed more and more distracted.

"You know, if anything's worrying you, I don't mind hearing about it," she said. She wished she could catch a glimpse of the usual sparkle in his brown eyes; it wasn't like Matt to stay this serious for so long.

He took his time answering. "Even if it's a business problem?" he asked finally.

"Well..." What should she say? She had a feeling that now wasn't the moment to tell him how certain she'd suddenly become about the two of them. She wanted to wait for the right opportunity, when he wasn't thinking of other things. Before that could happen, this matter of the phone calls needed to be resolved. "I don't mind, Matt. Not nearly as much as I mind wondering what's bothering you."

Matt sighed, and his mouth was a straight, serious line. "There *is* a problem, but I have no intention of bothering you with the details. And certainly no intention of working on it while we're supposed to be having a day off. But if you don't mind, I'd like to make one quick phone call while we're here. I won't be long."

Lily stayed in the conference room and let her eyes follow the rows of law volumes on the wall while Matt made the call from his private office. She wasn't trying to eavesdrop, but she did catch the occasional phrase. "I know she's upset, but I just can't do it this weekend. I can get to it first thing Monday, but right now I just need someone to go down there and talk the cops into letting the kid go home."

Clearly he wasn't getting what he wanted, and Lily could hear the mounting frustration in his voice. His sigh, when he hung up, was fully audible in the next room. But when he rejoined her, he was once again trying to act as though nothing were wrong.

"Why don't we go for a stroll around the town while it's still light?" she suggested. "And then maybe we can have dinner somewhere."

"Sounds good to me. How do you feel about seafood?"

"My father used to say I'd eat anything that swam," Lily said.

"Then we really are a match made in heaven."

If he'd said the words last night, Lily knew they would have sounded very different. But now, Matt sounded as though he were reading from a script. His part called for him to be the ardent lover, so he was saying all the right ardent lover-like things. But his heart wasn't in it—it was miles away in some legal world that Lily herself had told him she didn't want to share. She would have to set the record straight, she thought, just as soon as the right opportunity came up.

They'd only been walking for ten minutes when she was overtaken by the feeling that she couldn't spend the rest of the day like this. She stopped on a quiet street corner and turned to face him. "This is crazy, Matt," she said. "You're miserable because you can't be at work, and I'm miserable because you're miserable, and both of us are pretending we're having a good time."

His grin was weak, but at least he was smiling. "I guess you're right," he admitted, "but if you think I'm about to cave in and leave you alone—"

"Don't think about that," she ordered him. "Just tell me what's wrong, and let's take it from there."

Matt looked at her. Was she testing him, trying to find out how much he'd changed his style from the workaholic lawyer she'd rejected so adamantly? He'd do anything to convince her his work didn't rule his life anymore.

He hesitated so long that Lily spoke again. "If you're trying to figure out what I *want* you to say, forget it. I just want to know what's going on, pure and simple."

She had a point, Matt thought. He'd done a lousy job of hiding his concern over the phone calls, and if he couldn't cover up any better than that, then he should at least be honest about it.

"If it's any consolation, I'm not preoccupied thinking about some corporation that wants to swallow up some other corporation," he said. "I'm thinking about a fourteen-year-old boy who's in jail and scared out of his wits."

Lily's interest was immediate. "That's what the phone calls were about?"

"Yes. His mother is my secretary. They're as new in town as I am, and she didn't know anyone to call but me. I tried to find someone else to take care of it—that was the call I made from my office—but the one person I could think of is just on his way out of town."

"Why is the boy in jail?" Lily wanted to know.

"I'm not sure. His mother was so upset she didn't get around to leaving anything helpful like facts on my machine. She just kept saying that they wouldn't let Danny go and would I go down to the police station and talk to them."

Matt found himself breathing as hard as if he were in the middle of a marathon. This was the last big barrier, he knew, the one they had to get past if Lily was ever going to be his for good. "Come with me to the police station," he urged, "and you'll understand for yourself."

He saw her eyes widen, and he wondered again what she was thinking. *Bad enough to have to do business when they should have been spending time alone together, but to ask her to come with him...*

Her answer was the last one he'd expected. Taking him by the arm, she said, "All right. Let's get going, then." The next thing he knew she was propelling him back toward his

Jeep as though she couldn't understand what he was waiting for.

The evening passed like a series of images in a kaleido-
scope, shifting and disjointed. Matt fuming because everything took three times as long as he wanted it to. The arrival
of Matt's secretary, tearful and terrified that her only child
was about to be carried off to reform school. Interminable
interviews with police officers who'd taken the boy into
custody after he'd allegedly driven through someone's front
window in a stolen car. Forms, phone calls, more forms.
Lily knew it wasn't only lack of dinner that was making her
feel glazed by nine-thirty.

And then the whole scene suddenly acquired a focus when
Lily came out of the women's room to see a thin teenage boy
sitting on a bench in the waiting room. She looked around;
Matt and his secretary were talking with the police chief behind a counter. The boy was alone. He looked more tired
than Lily herself, and about four times as dejected.

Lily crossed the waiting room and sat a few feet away on
the same bench. "A person could grow roots waiting to get
out of here, huh?" she said companionably.

The boy smothered a yawn and nodded warily at her.
Something about him reminded Lily powerfully of herself
as a teenager. She'd gotten the impression from Matt that
there was no father in the picture, and she wondered if that
was what gave the boy the careful, cautious air she recognized so well. Maybe, as she had, he was having to grow up
depending on himself.

"My name's Lily," she said. "I'm a friend of Matt's."

The boy nodded again. "Danny," he said briefly.

Lily nodded back. A man of few words, she decided, but
brought up well enough to introduce himself to a stranger.

What to say next? "Does your mother work for Matt full-
time?" she asked, taking refuge in small talk.

He shook his head. "Three days a week," he said. "Two days a week she types at the high school. On weekends she does bookkeeping for people."

"That's quite a schedule."

Danny's mouth twisted. "She says she has to work that much," he said bitterly. "And she won't let me get a job." He clamped his jaws shut as if he'd said more than he'd meant to.

They sat in silence for a while, and then the boy turned tentatively to Lily. "What will they do to me, do you know?"

"I wish I could tell you," she said. "But it's impossible to say this early on. It depends on what the charge is and what the judge thinks of you."

"It would have to be the town manager's front window," Danny said, and Lily thought she saw a vague glimmer of humor in his face.

"Oh, dear," she said. "The town manager?" She tried to repress a smile and couldn't.

"I never did have very good luck." Danny was half smiling, too, and his thin fair face looked completely different. Then his smile faded. "Do you think I might get sent to reform school?"

Lily shrugged. "It's possible," she said, "but if you've never been in trouble before, I'd say it's unlikely."

Danny clenched his thin fists. "If I do—" he began, and then stopped. Lily could sense the frustration and anger he was grappling with, and she wished she could say something to reassure him. Matt would be good at that, she thought.

"I wish I knew what I should do," Danny said suddenly, and Lily looked at him more closely.

"Join the club," she said, trying to stay as low-key as she could. "What's worrying you?"

The boy leaned forward, forehead on his hands. "I'm not supposed to tell," he said in a muffled voice, "but if I have to go to reform school..."

"What aren't you supposed to tell?" Lily prodded gently.

He looked up. For a moment his mouth was pursed with indecision, and then he clearly made up his mind. "I wasn't driving that car," he said. "It was Kevin, he's a friend of mine."

"Did he tell the police you were driving?"

"No. I did."

"Why? You must have known what a lot of trouble it would be."

"I told you. Kevin's a friend of mine, and, well, he'd get in even bigger trouble than me."

"How come?"

"He's always getting into trouble, and his father always gets him out of it. But this time..."

Lily frowned, trying to piece things together. "How does his father get him off?" she asked.

Danny sighed. "His father's the town manager," he said.

"Oh, Lord." Now things were only too clear except for one important question. "Did you tell the police you were driving just so Kevin wouldn't get in trouble?"

He nodded. "Only I didn't really think about it, and now my mother's so upset, and if I have to go to reform school—"

"Will you tell the police the truth now?"

"But I promised Kevin."

"Would Kevin do the same thing for you in return?" Lily demanded.

Danny thought about it and then shook his head doubtfully.

"Then he doesn't deserve your promises. And if he's always getting in trouble, then your taking the blame this time isn't likely to keep him from getting in trouble again, is it?"

The head shake was more positive this time.

"I'll tell you something else. Matt is the best lawyer you could have, and he'll do everything he can for you, if you give him the truth to work with."

Once again there was hesitation on the boy's face. "Do I have to?" he asked.

"It's up to you," Lily said, hoping he'd come to the right answer on his own, without adult prompting.

"But if I tell . . ." His voice trailed off.

"Yes?" Lily's gentle voice was just above a whisper.

"I'm sort of scared of what Kevin might do."

"You think he might hurt you?"

"Maybe. Or he might . . . not be my friend any more."

It was Lily's turn to sigh. "Here's a piece of worldly advice for you, Danny, and you can take it or leave it, whichever you like. If you've got a hard decision to make, you shouldn't let being scared influence you. It's better to do what feels like the right thing, whether you're scared or not."

They were both silent for a while after Lily had spoken, and it would have been hard to say which of the two faces was more thoughtful.

"Here comes Matt," Lily said at last. "What do you think?"

"I think I'll tell him," Danny said. "Not about being scared, though."

He looked closely at Lily. "Don't worry," she said. "The part about being scared is just between you and me."

Matt knew it must be late when he woke up the next morning. The sun was shining aggressively into his bedroom, and he squinted into it, trying to figure out why he was so tired.

A few isolated facts drifted into his consciousness. It had been almost two in the morning by the time he and Lily had gotten home. Lily wasn't in bed with him now. From somewhere in the house he could hear the sound of a typewriter.

Those were all the facts he could manage. His eyelids drooped closed again, and he drifted on the edge of sleep as he tried to convince himself it was time to get up. The sound of typing made him think of his secretary, who came into his office on Mondays to type for him. If it was Monday, he wondered groggily, why was he still in bed?

Then he remembered. It was Monday, but he'd already announced his intention of taking the day off to spend it in romantic bliss with Lily. And instead he'd worked half the night and was now sleeping in by himself.

Now he was awake with a jolt. He rolled over on his back and said "Damn!" under his breath. Down the hall in his small office, Lily was busily typing something. He rubbed his eyelids, wishing they didn't feel so gritty. He'd slept badly all week, thinking inescapably of Lily. Moving to Brattleboro and setting up his new home and office had been hard work, too. And last night had finished the job on what was left of his stamina. If he wasn't so tired, he knew his mind would be functioning better than this.

He made himself review what had happened yesterday, starting with his secretary's first frantic message. "Danny's in trouble," she'd said, "and we need your help." His first, powerful reaction had been to dash off to the rescue, but he'd refused to let himself give in to that impulse. Hadn't Lily told him all along that he was too quick to let his work interfere with his private life?

Still Danny's problem hadn't seemed like work to Matt. These were people he knew, who needed his help. It had been impossible to put the phone messages out of his mind, and when Lily had unexpectedly agreed that he should go to the police station, he'd taken her up on it without a second's hesitation.

Had that been a mistake? He listened to the tapping of the typewriter and tried to figure out Lily's apparent change of heart. Maybe she'd come with him to Vermont to give their relationship one last try, and now that he'd proved himself to be just another lawyer who couldn't leave his work behind, she was actually relieved to have a final answer at last. Could that carefree mood of hers have been nothing more than relief at being done with Matt Malone and his problems?

That might explain some things, but not all of them. Matt wished he hadn't been so damned tired when they'd gotten home last night. He should have asked all these questions then. Snatches of their conversation on the way home floated through his mind.

"I don't know how you did it," he'd told her when they'd finally climbed into his Jeep and headed back to the cabin. "Danny swore up and down he'd been driving that car. I was pretty sure he wasn't telling the truth, but I couldn't get him to admit it."

"He seemed to want to tell somebody about it," Lily had said.

"To tell *you* about it, you mean. You sit there and look calm and serene and get more results than I do with all my jumping up and down."

"Maybe you should switch techniques, Mr. Malone."

"It's a thought, Ms. Martineau. Although thanks to your technique, I'm now officially starting my career in Brattleboro by accusing the town manager's son of auto theft and malicious damage to his father's house."

"Good thing you love a fight, huh?"

"If I hadn't loved fighting, I never would have gotten this far with you," he'd replied, but the conversation had taken another turn before he could find out just how far he *had* gotten.

Or had he gotten nowhere at all? He rolled back over on his side, rubbing his eyes. What was she writing that was so official it needed to be typed? The thought struck him that it must be a goodbye letter, telling him he'd had his final chance and had blown it. She'd seemed so interested in Danny last night, and so sympathetic to the whole problem. But maybe that didn't really change anything. Maybe she'd decided once and for all that Matt wasn't the man for her.

That thought was unbearable. Matt threw aside the down comforter and got out of bed, determined to find out what she was doing. If she'd been typing up her side of *Malone versus Martineau*, he didn't know what he could say or do to talk her out of it this time.

Lily switched off Matt's small electronic typewriter and finished reading over what she'd just typed. She couldn't make things any clearer than that, she thought. If Matt wanted to be a lawyer through and through, then he deserved to have legal documents thrown at him first thing in the morning.

She smiled and tucked her bare feet under her. The day was sunny but cold, and she hadn't bothered to look for her slippers when she'd left the bedroom. The warmth from her thick blue flannel nightgown took the chill from her toes.

She wondered if it was still too early to wake Matt. He'd been so tired when they'd finally arrived home that she could see the accumulated stress in his eyes. He'd poured them both a drink, but hadn't finished half by the time he fell asleep in a chair. "Some host," he'd mumbled when she'd gently roused him and steered him into the bedroom.

Well, let him sleep. He'd worked hard enough last night for two lawyers. Calling the town manager and his son at ten o'clock had been above and beyond the call of duty, she knew, but Matt had insisted it was better to strike while the iron was hot. And he'd been right. Surprised by Matt's call, Danny's friend Kevin had mumbled and hedged and finally admitted to what he'd done.

"Catching the witness off guard, are you?" she'd asked him.

"Sometimes it works," he assured her, and she could see he was right. Her own first impulse was to retreat and go

about things gently; Matt's was to charge in with all flags
flying. Between the two of them, they'd managed to keep
the whole business in balance last night and sort things out
for Danny and his mother.

Keeping things in balance. That was the phrase that kept
coming back to Lily the next morning. Finally she'd gotten
out of bed, leaving Matt sleeping soundly, and gone in
search of a paper and pen—or better yet, a typewriter—to
put her thoughts in order. Now she'd done it, and she was
pleased with the result. She lowered her feet from the chair,
put the pages in order and padded back into the bedroom.

She met Matt at the door. "Why the frown?" she asked,
taking in his lowered eyebrows and tousled hair. "It's too
nice a day to be looking so serious."

Matt didn't care whether it was a nice day or not. All his
attention was focused on Lily, and her smile took him by
surprise. She didn't look as though she'd just been writing
a farewell note to end a misguided love affair. Why, then,
the official-looking typed pages in her hand, neatly held
with a paper clip?

His frown deepened. He had to get to the bottom of this,
but at the moment all he could think of was how lovely Lily
looked, and how bereft he'd felt when he'd wakened and
found himself alone. In her simple blue nightgown, with her
dark hair still tangled by sleep, she had an unusual glow
about her, and Matt couldn't resist it.

He gave up trying and pulled her into his arms. The
warm, sweet scent of her surrounded him as he kissed the
base of her neck. "I'm not frowning just at the moment,"
he said, "and I promise I won't frown anymore if you come
back to bed with me."

Lily smiled. "What do you think I was on my way to
do?" she asked. Her smile widened as he picked her up and
carried her back to the bed. They lay together on the rumpled comforter, lost in the familiar heart-quickening urge of
desire they could each feel in the other.

"I thought you might be on your way to give me my walking papers," Matt said, looking closely at her.

Lily raised herself until she sat cross-legged beside him. "Not exactly," she said. She still wore that satisfied smile, and it was driving Matt crazy.

"I can't hold you if you're going to sit like that," he complained, and tried to draw her back into his arms.

"That's the idea." Lily stayed sitting up with the typed pages in her hand. "This is serious, Matt, so listen."

"I'm listening." He compromised by laying his head on her lap.

He was so handsome, she thought. Even unshaven, with slight dark circles under his eyes, he could make her heart turn over just by looking at her. Everything about him was so alive. She ran her hand gently through his auburn hair, and her mind started to wander to thoughts of making love. But she made herself concentrate; after all, they had business to transact here.

"This is a draft of the case of *Malone* versus *Martineau*," she began. Instantly he frowned, and she put out a hand to trace the lines in his forehead. "I thought you weren't going to frown anymore if I came back to bed," she said.

"And I thought *Malone* versus *Martineau* was a thing of the past," he replied. Could she really be intending to end things, with that look on her face? It didn't make any sense.

"Just listen. 'Whereas—'"

"'Whereas'? You're hitting me with 'whereas' first thing in the morning?"

"It's nearly eleven, so no sympathy for you, buster." She cleared her throat. "'Whereas Lily Martineau will shortly be without a job and is officially ending the search for a law firm specializing in the kind of work she wants—'"

"What do you mean, ending the search? What are you going to do, file insurance reports for the rest of your life?"

"Just listen. 'And whereas Matthew Malone, on November 9, made a proposal that the said Lily Martineau should enter into partnership in his legal firm—'"

"And was turned down in no uncertain terms," Matt reminded her, but she ignored him.

"'And whereas the said Lily Martineau has since that time received new information about the said Matthew Malone—'"

"What new information?" Matt was sitting up straighter now, leaning on one elbow.

"I'm coming to that. 'The said new information consisting of three parts: (a) that the said Lily Martineau was acting on insufficient evidence in assuming that all lawyers were tarred with the same brush, (b) that the said Matthew Malone does, in fact, share the said Lily Martineau's ideas and feelings about the law, and (c)—'" Lily's voice became a little less glib "'—that the said Lily Martineau is in love with the said Matthew Malone.'" She cleared her throat, then continued, "'Therefore, she proposes that they enter into the partnership suggested by Matthew Malone on November 9, in a legal sense and whatever other sense seems appropriate to both parties.'"

She clipped the pages back together. For all her businesslike air, her heart was pounding so hard it made her fingers shake.

Matt's heart was beating fast, too. "Lily, I know I'm a lawyer," he said, "and I'm not supposed to say this, but could you explain that to me in real words?"

Lily brushed back a strand of hair that had fallen across her face. "In real words, I'm saying I've changed my mind," she said. "Matt, I've been so stubborn ever since last summer. I think I honestly believed that any lawyer who took a business call after five o'clock was married to his job."

"There are lots who are; I used to be one of them."

"Yes, and there are also lots who fall somewhere in between, and I think you're one of those now. When I saw how good you were with Danny last night, I realized just how much you must have been wanting to do this kind of law—helping people out, not just engineering corporate takeovers. And of course there are cases where you have to give up your free time. Last night was one of them. And it wasn't just seeing you at work last night. It was the way I felt when I saw you at the art show in Hartford. I knew then that I'd been waiting for the wrong kind of evidence about you."

"What kind were you waiting for?"

"Something to convince me you'd never put a legal case ahead of a personal one, I guess. Something that wasn't very realistic. But when I saw you in Hartford, I knew I already had the evidence I needed in here."

She put her free hand against her chest, and Matt put one of his hands over it. "That was the evidence I was operating on all along," he said.

"I know, and you can say 'I told you so' if you want to."

He didn't seem to want to. He leaned forward, and the strength of his body pushed her back among the pillows. "I don't suppose you've noticed, but it's impossible for me to hold you like this and not want to make love with you."

"I did notice," she smiled, "but we're supposed to be working on a legal document just at the moment."

"That's a switch," he commented. The warm caress of his lips almost put an end to her resolve, and as he kissed her he could feel her whole body springing into life in response. There was such a vibrancy deep inside whenever Matt touched her. Was it more like burning or melting? She could never quite decide. And now she would have a long, long time to think it over and make the choice.

"Well?" she said when he raised his lips from hers at last.

"Well, what?" There was a rasp of satisfaction in his voice.

"Well, do you want to sign my contract and make it official?"

He kept one arm tightly around her as they sat up. "I'd like to make a change to the last paragraph," he said. "Let's delete this vague business of 'whatever other sense seems appropriate to both parties,' and include a wedding date instead."

Lily couldn't help the grin that spread across her face. Even now, she couldn't quite believe this was going to come true. "All right," she said. "Let me just get a pencil and add that in."

"Oh, no, you don't!" Matt held her forcibly against him. "You're not getting away that easily." In case she had any doubts about his sincerity, he kissed her again. That kiss very nearly ended the discussion and threatened to lead on to other things, but Matt had one more thing to say. He lifted his lips from hers, but only barely, so that Lily could still feel the touch of his breath. "I thought I'd lost you for good, when I woke up this morning," he said. "I thought dragging you with me to the police station might have been the biggest mistake I ever made."

Lily shook her head. "You didn't drag me, if you recall," she told him. "And anyway, aside from helping Danny, it helped me some, too. It was while I was talking to Danny that I realized just how scared I'd been about having my heart broken again and that being scared had colored everything I'd always felt about you. I gave Danny some advice on that subject, advice I'd already decided to take, myself. It's like—like Tommy Thompson, in a way. You just have to make a habit of getting right back up whenever something knocks you down."

"Think we should invite her to the wedding?" Matt's voice was muffled as he kissed the long line of her neck and ended up at the little spot he knew so well at the base of her ear.

Lily shivered all over, longing for his touch. She was rapidly losing interest in Tommy and in everything else but the way Matt's hands were outlining her body through the warm layer of her nightgown. "Sure," she said breathlessly, "although she'll probably assault an usher and wind up taking us to court."

"Who'll defend her, you or me?"

"It doesn't matter. We're on the same side now, remember?"

Matt remembered. He was reminding her of it as persuasively as only he could, and when Lily let *Malone* versus *Martineau* drop over the side of the bed, neither one of them seemed in a hurry to go after it and pick it up again.

*   *   *   *   *

The heat wave coming your way has arrived...

⬥ SILHOUETTE SUMMER *Sizzlers*

Whether in the sun or on the run, take a mini-vacation with these three original stories in one compact volume written by three top romance authors—

Nora Roberts
Parris Afton Bonds
Kathleen Korbel

Indulge yourself in steamy romantic summertime reading—

Summer was never so sizzling!

Available NOW!

SIZ-1B

You'll flip . . . your pages won't!
Read paperbacks *hands-free* with

Book Mate · I

The perfect "mate" for all your romance paperbacks

**Traveling • Vacationing • At Work • In Bed • Studying
• Cooking • Eating**

Perfect size for all standard paperbacks, this wonderful invention makes reading a pure pleasure! Ingenious design holds paperback books OPEN and FLAT so even wind can't ruffle pages – leaves your hands free to do other things. Reinforced, wipe-clean vinyl-covered holder flexes to let you turn pages without undoing the strap . . . supports paperbacks so well, they have the strength of hardcovers!

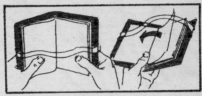

Pages turn WITHOUT opening the strap

SEE-THROUGH STRAP

Reinforced back stays flat

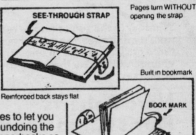

Built in bookmark

BOOK MARK

BACK COVER HOLDING STRIP

10″ x 7¼″, opened.
Snaps closed for easy carrying, too